W9-AMX-071

AFRICAN WRITERS SERIES
Editorial Adviser · Chinua Achebe

61
The Way
We Lived

AFRICAN WRITERS SERIES

REMS NNA UMEASIEGBU

The Way We Lived

IBO CUSTOMS AND STORIES

JUN 4 '71

HEINEMANN EDUCATIONAL BOOKS

LONDON · IBADAN · NAIROBI

Heinemann Educational Books Ltd
48 Charles Street, London W1X 8AH
PMB 5205, Ibadan · POB 25080, Nairobi
MELBOURNE TORONTO AUCKLAND
HONG KONG SINGAPORE

SBN 435 90061–7

Illustrations and cover
by Peter Edwards

Printed in Malta
by St Paul's Press

Contents

Part 2   Folklore

For my parents

TO MY FATHER
MR G. U. UMEASIEGBU

Oxfordshire
Christmas 1966

My dear Father

I wonder if you still remember the second Sunday of March 1953? On this particular day you were entertaining some councillors of the now Aba Urban County Council. You reprimanded me seriously in the presence of your guests. You even threatened to withdraw me from school. It was my fault I know, but do you still remember the incident? I shall tell you.

I served wine to your friends and handed them their glasses without sipping the wine. You deplored my action and urged me to learn the Ibo customs within two months – otherwise you would withdraw me from school.

Within the next two months I had learnt most of the customs. So interesting and enthralling were they that I spent the next ten years studying the customs and everything connected with the Ibo heritage. The Way We Lived *is the result of such a study and you have helped me and a good number of people who may read this book.*

I am very, very grateful, Sir.
Your dutiful son,
Rems

Preface

Nigeria includes the Hausa, Kanuri, Fulani, Nupe, Tiv, Yoruba, Edo, Ibo, Ibibio and Annang tribes. The first five are in the Northern part of the country, while the rest are in the South. There are other minor peoples but these are the chief ones. Each of them is an indigenous tribe. The area lived in by the Ibos is small compared with the lands lived in by some other tribes. The Ibos live in Port Harcourt, Owerri, Umuahia, Abakaliki, Ogoja, Onitsha and Enugu. They number between five and seven million people and the people are known for their zeal, hard work and consequent progress. No work is too small or too big. They have made their lands fertile. Food crops include yam, palm oil and nuts, cassava and fruits of various kinds.

Practically all the customs detailed in this book are now obsolete and are nowhere to be found amongst the Ibo today. They have been put down here for record purposes. The rate at which changes are being effected in our society is alarming. There is no doubt that in time things that have a great vogue now will be classified as out-moded; it will be sad if our colourful and rich legacy is lost in this rather cut-throat rush towards 'civilization'.

My own father was mainly responsible for the 'hand-over' to me of the customs and ways of life of our ancestors, but I strongly doubt if I shall have the patience, interest and common sense to sit down and narrate the accounts to my own children. My children, therefore, are not likely to know any of these gifts so freely given and their offspring will never know them either. In this way the legacy will be lost.

It is with these views in mind that I have attempted to

record as many as I can remember. Any student of Ibo language or culture will realize that discrepancies must always occur in two different works of this type. By 'different', I mean two versions given by two different authors. An illustration will make this clear: take the breaking of kola nut as an example. In Awka – a district about forty-three miles to the north-east of Onitsha practices differ. In some places the oldest member of the group breaks the kola nut, whereas in other parts of the district the youngest member breaks the nut.

As far as possible I shall try to locate the differences and similarities by giving specific examples.

To avoid monotony, I have changed some of the names of the characters of the fables. It does not make good reading if the tortoise appears as the principal character in all the stories. The animals in the stories are all personified and you will find the sheep being addressed as Mrs Sheep, etc. Almost all the stories have a lesson to teach. Some go to show that it pays to be honest and kind; others are told for the rhythmic music they produce and others mix up the beliefs of the people over certain natural phenomena: for example, why hawks carry chicks. The colourful details of the fables have been slightly modified in my attempt to avoid direct translations from the Ibo versions as I know them.

I am happy to express my gratitude to: Mr Emma O. Monube and Mr Dominic Umeasiegbu for their encouragement and advice on some important details; to Mr Chinua Achebe for his extremely helpful comments; to Mr and Mrs G. U. Umeasiegbu, without whose help this book could never have been written.

Rems Umeasiegbu

Part I

Customs

1 *A first child in the family*

A married couple is looked upon with contempt if the marriage is not solidified with a child. The first prayer on the lips of all couples, therefore, is that God will give them children. Newly married maidens are advised to be kind to children. As soon as the lady becomes pregnant, jubilation starts in the family. When her pregnancy enters the sixth or seventh month, her mother-in-law comes to stay with her. She advises the expectant mother to refrain from hard work. Food is prepared and served to her.

As soon as her labour is about to start she is taken to a native doctor or to a hospital if there is one. When the baby is born the proud mother-in-law trots off to break the good news to her son. She sings and dances on the way and passers-by join her. The happy and proud father of the baby picks up his dane-gun and fires two shots in the air. The number of shots is increased if the baby is a boy. He brings kegs of fresh palm wine, kola nuts, alligator pepper and dried tapioca, and the well-wishers – mainly women – help themselves. They sing and dance in mad ecstasy and implore their ancestors to thank God on their behalf for increasing the number of people in their village. Songs of praise are sung in honour of the father, who has now attained manhood. Manhood is assessed by a man's ability to make his wife pregnant. If he cannot, he is reckoned a 'half-man'.

The team, headed by the jubilant mother-in-law, sets off for the house of the child's grandfather. He must have heard of his fortune for no sooner has he seen the surging crowd of women than he fires a number of gunshots into the air. He is greeted by all present and is implored to be up and doing for he has seen a grandchild. His merriment is all the more joyous if the child is his first grandchild. Palm wine, alligator pepper and all the other accessories also feature prominently. He brings out cohise chalk which everyone present must use. They all paint their foreheads, hands, ankles and elbows with it. Drumming starts and the well-wishers dance and sway – some dancing to the tune, others dancing any way they like. Meanwhile, someone has gone to narrate the story to the mother of the lady who has given birth to the child. She walks as fast as her legs can carry her in order to join the party.

The dancers are given gifts of money. Coins are stamped on their foreheads. These coins are often no bigger than a farthing or a penny. The proud grandparents sit at the centre and sip palm wine now and then from their drinking horns. All roads now lead to this spot. Every villager who hears the good news comes to express his happiness. The length of time spent here depends on how well the child's grandfather has treated them. If he is a wealthy man he may wish to display his opulence by ordering some bottles of illicit gin, or even beer and mineral drinks. The next place the party calls at is the home of the lady who has the new child. Here, her father is already holding a party. Everyone drinks once again. Songs of praise are given for all the members of the two families. The party then ends with a prayer that God will continue to give them more children. Every person goes away to come back in two days' time when the lady and her child will be back. This time they come with all sorts of gifts – items of clothing, toilet requirements, food, drinks and money. One or two may even volunteer to spend a day or two doing the domestic work for the new mother.

2 Breaking a kola nut

In Iboland much importance is attached to kola nuts. If an Ibo man visits a fellow Ibo, he does not feel he is a welcome visitor until his host offers him kola. What normally happens is that the host shakes hands with his guests and ushers them to their seats. They talk generally for a few minutes before the host takes leave of them and enters his private room. He comes back with an old leather bag flung over his shoulder. The bag is opened and a piece of kola nut is brought out. Having touched it with his lips, the host hands it to the oldest man among his guests. The object of 'kissing' the kola nut is to prove to those present that he has given the kola in good faith and that it does not contain any poison, the argument being that if the nut does contain poison, the host will be the first to die. If he does not touch the kola with his lips, it will be rejected.

The oldest man then shows it to everyone present and each of them records his approval by touching the nut which is now being passed round. The oldest member of the team then breaks it saying as he cuts it in pieces:

'Live and let live; may we live long in order to see our great grandchildren.'

Those present respond by saying 'Amen.'

Another may join in with: 'He who brings kola brings life.'

The pieces of kola are passed round by the youngest among them; everyone partakes of it. Kola nut is always offered whether or not the host knows the guests are coming. In some places the youngest person breaks the kola instead of the oldest. In most parts of Awka, the duty falls on the oldest, but in Ngwaland, more often than not it is the responsibility of the youngest among them.

3

If palm wine is to be served, the youngest serves it. It is never served by the oldest. If the wine is being served by a member of the host's family, then such a person must drink a glassful first; if he does not drink he must sip it. If – on the other hand – it is poured out by one of the guests, the server hands a glassful to the host first. The object again is to make sure that it is harmless to drink. If there is a woman among them she drinks the wine kneeling down. If she is an elderly woman, say fifty years old, she drinks sitting down, like her male counterparts. On no account is wine ever served by a female. The last glass of wine is handed to the host. If the server makes a mistake about this, he is ordered to buy a gallon of wine as his punishment. The host either drinks the wine or gives it to the oldest man among them.

3 *Burial of a titled man*

The type of burial given to a dead man depends primarily on his social status when he was alive. Wealthy men, chiefs, titled men and warriors, are buried with pomp and pageantry, but poor and insignificant men without any incidents. As soon as a titled man falls ill, all the titled men in his area make a contribution which is given to his wives and children. This money is used in buying him things he wants. Medicine-men of renown are paid to take care of him. The titled man may fashion his own grave and order his own coffin, or he may give instructions to his children.

As soon as he dies, the Ukoro (a gigantic wooden drum whose sound can travel about ten miles) is beaten. An interval of at least ten minutes elapses before the next sound. This signifies the death of someone important. The villagers rush towards the direction of the sound. If the chief or titled man had been ill for a long time, the people will immediately know that he is now dead. Young men are sent to different villages in search of human heads. It is generally believed that a titled man or a chief must always be buried with human heads – otherwise he will not be given a rousing reception in the lower world. Young men are honoured and awarded titles if they are successful in bringing home these heads. Often too, they are given the privilege to choose any spinster in the whole village for a wife. In some parts of Iboland heads of animals are preferred to human heads, but places such as Bende Division and some parts of Ngwaland insist on human heads.

The corpse is washed, powdered and scented and dressed in a chieftain's regalia. It is placed on a well-decorated sofa. Two of his servants or slaves stand at the back of the sofa. Sympathizers are allowed to come in and pay their last respects. If he was a native doctor or medicine-man during his lifetime, his tools of trade are placed in the coffin. When the heads are brought, they are placed at each side of the coffin and the coffin is carried by four of his servants. He may be buried in front of his house or in one of his rooms, depending on the instructions he gave when he was alive. If he is buried in front of his house, a shrub is planted at the centre of the grave for remembrance' sake. It is the eldest son of the family who first throws sand over the coffin. The crowd disperses to come back in four days' time for the waking and funeral ceremonies.

4 Circumcision

Circumcision is one of the conditions that must be fulfilled before marriage. Whenever a woman comes back from the place where she was delivered of her baby, arrangements for the child's circumcision start. Circumcision is invariably the first of the rites to be accorded the new-born baby. It is usually fixed for the eighth day after the birth of the baby.

There are women who specialize in this work. It is the practice to look for a woman who has a good record in her job. There is no point in getting someone who causes extreme loss of blood or causes much pain to the child. A further qualification is that she must have given birth to at least three children. Circumcision conducted by a woman who has no children – according to popular opinion – takes a long time to heal. On the eighth day the circumcisor arrives. Bandages, razor blades and a pair of scissors; a small towel, stock-fish, a roll of tobacco are all required and must be ready for the circumcisor's use.

Her requirements are shown to her and she instructs the child's mother to boil some water for her. If the mother is a young lady she is not allowed to stay: in which case, a fairly old woman from the neighbourhood is asked to come and help. This woman sits down and takes the baby on her lap. The circumcisor comes in and shuts the door. Men are never allowed to come in during the operation.

With the brand new blades she adroitly carries out her duty. She washes the baby with warm water and applies fresh palm oil to the part affected. The parents of the child are allowed in now and they give the woman a stipend of two shillings and sixpence. The woman in turn gives threepence or sixpence to the other companion who carried the baby during the process. She gives a can of palm oil which is to be applied frequently to the affected part. The used materials – blades, towel and cotton swabs – are buried. She goes away with the stockfish and the tobacco roll. Daily visits are paid to the family in order to ascertain the child's progress, or otherwise. Her popularity and prestige are enhanced if sepsis does not set in.

If for any reason, an Ibo is not circumcised during child-hood, he must do so before marriage. Failure to do so may wreck his marriage.

5 *Cohise chalk*

Cohise chalk has several uses, but by far its most important use is in the worshipping of gods and idols. Pagans use it because of its sacredness. Before a worshipper talks to his god in the morning, he must first of all draw a large circle with the chalk and make some sketches on the statue of the god with this chalk. His sacrifice is null and void if he does not start his offering with cohise chalk.

Any woman who gives birth to a child makes an extensive use of this clayey chalk. She gives the chalk to every one of her visitors. The visitor draws some lines on her forehead, arms and ankles, signifying her happiness at her friend's good luck. When her baby is old enough to be taken to the market square, she takes many pieces of the chalk with her. All her well-wishers will demand a piece, which will be returned to her afterwards. Some may decide to make gifts to her with cohise chalk. In this sense, therefore, cohise chalk symbolizes joyousness.

It can also be used as kola. Some people prefer to give the chalk first to their visitors before bringing out the real kola nut. A few fastidious guests may insist on being presented with it before the actual nut. All good hosts always have cohise chalk stored away for use in emergency.

The last use of the chalk is as a danger signal. Any place that is out of bounds is encircled with cohise chalk to warn trespassers of the danger.

Whichever way it is used, the truth remains that cohise chalk is an indispensable household item.

6 *Divorce in Iboland*

There are many conditions to be fulfilled before a young man takes a wife. At times he has to suffer one or two humiliations or he may have to perform an extremely dangerous task before he is considered fit for marriage. This goes to make divorce very rare in Iboland. If a man wants to get married he must be able to convince his parents that he is qualified. He sets about looking for the right girl. His friends will help him. When he finds the girl he carries casks of palm wine to the prospective father-in-law who may request him to come and work for a number of days on his farm. This is to test him in order to find out if he is hard-working or not.

It is not surprising then, that divorce is something that should always be abhorred. If a dispute arises in the family, the couple invites some members of both families and a couple of friends. Each of them states the grounds of complaint. The invitees decide the case and cautions whoever is at fault.

There are certain things that can wreck a hitherto happy marriage, one of which is marital infidelity. If a man catches his wife with another man, he demands an immediate divorce. As usual, members of both families are summoned, and some friends too. Casks of palm wine are brought. Tobacco is provided for the old men and women, who may resort to heavy and long pipe-smoking.

In clear terms the husband tells the people why he has summoned them. The wife gives her own version of the story. Investigations are carried out and the people all come back in a few days' time. If it is proved that the wife has been a flirt, the marriage is declared null and void. The man gives an account of how much money he has spent on the wife, including the dowry paid. The wife's family gives him the assurance that the money will be paid in full as soon as the wife re-marries. If she does not get a new husband, the money cannot be recovered; but if she does, the man claims back his money.

7 Getting ready for marriage

The birth of a baby girl carries special responsibilities. Just as the mother of the baby girl remained a virgin until the day she was married, so also is the daughter expected to remain a virgin till such time as she is married. It is the sacred duty of the mother to instruct and guide her daughter so that she may not fall a victim to the traps set by men. If a girl becomes pregnant before she is traditionally married, she is treated as an outcast and her presence is a bad omen. Her mother in turn, is looked upon as an irresponsible sex-maniac.

For this reason, special precautions are taken. As soon as a girl attains the age of puberty, she is taken to a specially equipped room, known as the 'Fattening room'. Here she spends seven market days (twenty-eight days). She does nothing other than eating and sleeping. She is locked up in this room and meals are served to her there. Her mother is the only woman who is allowed to enter her room. She has five meals daily. Every morning her mother goes to her and gives her a tepid bath. Uhie Awusa (a mixture of red clayey soil and oil) and Uli (juice obtained from the fruit of a tree that grows wild in the gardens) are lavishly used. This juice rubbed on the body, remains colourless and hidden only to give black colouration to the parts of the body touched with the liquid. This black colouration appears after thirty hours and remains indelible for a week or so. Both of them are used to produce intricate designs on the girl's body. On her breasts are drawn a mother and a little child. The significance of this is to drive home to the girl that those breasts of hers should be used to feed her baby when she gets one. The idea of feeding a baby with animal milk is strongly condemned.

The maiden's body looks as slippery as that of a fish and her voice becomes very sonorous. She starts to put on weight. She may develop a 'moon' face. On the whole she becomes more beautiful than she was before going into the fattening room. Sleep occupies most of her time – about fifteen hours daily. Two hours of her time may be spent dreaming, thinking of the man she will meet when she comes out and the frivolities and enjoyments of life. Four to five hours may be spent eating and the rest spent at her toilet table.

Meanwhile, news is circulating that a pretty maiden is due to leave the fattening room soon. Her last day in this room will coincide with the village's market day. In the evening, members of her age-group come to escort her to the market square. Her waist is adorned with multi-coloured beads and her virgin breasts sway from side to side in order to attract eligible bachelors. Her eye-brows are painted coal black and everything about her is nothing but beauty.

She goes from one stall to another and gifts are made to her. She does not touch any of them; it is the work of the girls escorting her. She keeps mute but acknowledges the gifts with a smile. Members of her age-group bring her home after they have gone round the market.

From now onwards she is ready for marriage.

8 *Hunting*

Hunting is a favourite pastime among the Ibos and it is also a lucrative occupation. The game includes giraffes, lions, tigers, leopards, monkeys, antelopes, ostriches, and at times, elephants. Hunters do not go on hunting trips individually. There are a great many animals that a hunter, no matter how experienced, can never kill alone. Moreover, some animals go in groups. There are two classes of hunters – the amateurs and the professionals. Each of these classes organizes its own trips. Each group has a dozen men and a particular zone is allocated to it.

Four days before the hunting trip, the spokesman for the group will announce in the market square that their group will

*A young maiden being escorted
to the market square*

go on a hunting expedition. He gives the time and tells them the meeting place. Each member has to provide himself with gunpowder. On the appointed day they all assemble, each with his dog. These dogs wear locally manufactured bells around their necks, the object being to make their movements known to the hunters. They set off on their journey when they have completed all arrangements. On arrival at the zone of operation, they sit down to take a little snuff. The trained dogs are now sent to different directions. If it is night-time, they do not come with their dogs and each hunter will have to carry a headlamp.

The noise of the bells around the dogs' necks will scare off the animals and in fear they run about the jungle. The hunters, now in readiness, carry their dane-guns very firmly. As soon as the animals run across their path, these hunters shoot. At times, the dogs kill little animals themselves. At the end of the day's hunting trip they all go back home to share their booty. If a hunter mistakenly shoots a fellow-hunter, such a person is suspended and his gun confiscated for a period of twenty market days – i.e. eighty days.

9 Marrying a new wife

When a young man thinks he is ready to take a wife he goes to his parents and makes his intentions known to them. If his parents are no longer living, he confides in his nearest relative. His father will find out how much money he has. If he is financially resourceful and stable (and provided he is of age) his father will approve the plan. The latter invites his friends and relatives and tells them of his son's noble plan to rear a family of his own. He charges them with the duty of looking for a young girl, who is still a virgin and whose character is untarnished.

The friends and relations go home and start making enquiries. Any beautiful girl seen is questioned and her family history and background found out. If they feel such a girl will make an ideal housewife, they inform the prospective suitor. He is shown the girl and if she appeals to him, the secret is divulged to the girl. The man informs his father of his friends' success and the girl in turn informs her parents. The girl's parents are told when the suitor and his family and friends are coming.

On the appointed day, four gallons of palm wine are bought. Other purchases include snuff, rolls of tobacco, powder and cream. In the evening the party sets off for the girl's house. On arrival they will be ushered in by the girl's father. He presents his guests with kola. After this has been served, the prospective groom's father presents the four gallons of wine. As the drinking progresses the people group themselves and engage in little talks. Their conversation will range from the day's activities to the influence of the white man in the society. When it appears everyone is sober again, one of the elders accompanying the husband-to-be starts talking in proverbs. As soon as every person has understood the purpose of the mission, the hostess serves rice, foo-foo and yams.

After the plates have been cleared, the man calls his daughter. She appears, putting on an air of indifference. All eyes are now focused on her. A glass is filled with wine and handed to her. She has two alternatives, either to give it to her father or to her husband-to-be, after sipping it. If she gives it to the suitor, it means she has accepted him. If she does otherwise, then the matter ends there. After she has accepted the young man, her father asks her to go away. The dowry is discussed. A lot of bargaining takes place now. If the two families cannot arrive at a compromise, the meeting becomes a failure; but if a compromise is arrived at, the young man pays the money. If he has not got it with him he names a date when he will come back to pay. When they are ready to go, the girl is called and asked to carry one of the empty casks to her husband's house. She spends a day or two with the husband's mother.

The following morning, the mother-in-law will give her about ten shillings to go to market to buy ingredients for making soup. If she spends the ten shillings, she is termed extravagant and the husband may demand his dowry back. If, on the other hand, she brings back change, she is praised. When she is ready to go back to her father's house, she is given some presents, such as beads, ear-rings, necklaces and bangles. A cask of wine is bought for her father. When she leaves her father's house finally for her new home, her parents give her gifts. Bicycles, sewing-machines and cooking utensils are among the commonest gifts given to newly-married girls.

10 *Moonlight plays*

Night-time is a period for relaxation, amusement and social get-together. When a new phase of the moon starts, everyone is delighted and offers thanks to God. With the aid of the moon's light the people are all able to gather at a rendezvous which is either a part of the market place or the chief's palace. Every night, for as long as the moon continues to give out its light, the villagers come together. In the evenings, the meeting place is swept clean. Children work hard to see that they discharge their domestic duty before the emergence of the moon.

Around seven in the evening the ekwe (a little drum) is sounded to declare that the preparations have been completed. All roads now lead to the chief's palace, or wherever the people are expected for the plays. Boys and girls group themselves; old men and women sit apart and the middle-aged have a place for themselves. Every villager is expected to turn up, excepting perhaps, the invalid and the aged. The elders resort to pipe smoking. They give their endless stocks of proverbs and stories while children sit tongue-tied, their eyes glued to the story-teller's mouth.

A few other children however, may like to be left alone. They organize various plays. Dancing and drumming may feature prominently too. For all, it is a prized opportunity for meeting and chatting with members of their age-groups. The older ones use it as an opportunity for love-making. Boys see it as a chance to woo girls of their choice. If a chief has any important pronouncement to make, everyone is summoned to come closer to the raised dais where he normally sits. One of the attendants is responsible for keeping the time. Towards midnight he sounds the ekwe. This reminds those present that it is time to disperse. Six stout men then patrol the grounds to see that no-one is left behind.

11 *Mourning for a dead husband*

As soon as a married man becomes ill, friends and relatives are told. They, with his wife, are responsible for his medical treatment and comfort. He may be taken to a hospital or a medicine-man. The wife is particularly worried and does all in her power to help her husband. If all attempts to save his life fail and he finally dies, all his children are asked to come home unless they reside overseas. These sons and daughters come home to pay their last respects to their father.

The wife brushes her hair clean and changes her clothing. Instead of putting on any sort of dress she likes, she is instructed to use deep black mourning dresses. It is a serious offence if she is ever seen using a material which is not black for her clothing. No matter where she is going, she must put on black dresses. After a period of six months she is allowed to use any other colour she chooses.

For the first week following the bereavement, she remains indoors. Neighbours and sympathizers bring food to her because she is not allowed to cook. If she is an unpopular woman she may not get the complete three meals daily. She relies exclusively on the generosity or benevolence of her late husband's relatives. She does not talk to any man unless such a man comes from either of the two families. At the end of the mourning period she has to decide whether to re-marry or not. If she has already had a child, she may not re-marry. In this case, if she insists on getting a new husband, one of her late husband's brothers takes her as one of his wives. Generally she is free to remain a widow and invite men of her choice to keep her company.

When a baby is old enough to be carried on the mother's back, the parents make arrangements for the naming ceremony. A day is fixed and a handful of friends and relations are invited. Different dishes are prepared by the baby's grandmother, who has been nursing both the baby and its mother. Rice, garri, yam and foo-foo are all prepared. Stockfish, ordinary fish and meat abound in the soup and stew. Benches are arranged in a rectangular fashion and at the centre stands a bush-lamp, (the ceremony is always held at night).

When the guests arrive they are ushered in by the baby's mother whose first public engagement this is since the delivery of the baby. Kola nuts are served, followed by palm wine. When the hostess feels satisfied that everyone has had enough to drink, she gives instructions to her mother to bring the food. The mother in turn, sends the servants with the trays of food. The guests choose whichever food they want – rice, garri, foo-foo or yam. More wine is served and the hostess urges her guests to wash down the food with plenty of wine. The servants are called to clear the tables after the meal.

The host gives one or two proverbs and orders the baby to be brought. He takes it on his lap. It is now evident that the naming ceremony has started. It is the baby's grandmother who suggests a name first. The father then gives his after which the mother gives hers. There are many names to be chosen from, but a name that has been given already to a member of the family, is never given. If the baby has many brothers and sisters, it may be named Adaobi (daughter of the family) or Obigeli (person sent to enjoy the fruits and blesssings of the family); the names of the market days may be given:

Nwafor, Nwoye, Nwankwo and Nwaorie; other names are thought of depending on the circumstances surrounding the baby's birth. Thus we have such names as Udodi (there is peace), Asieme (implementing decisions), Nwakaego (a child is better than money), Ngozi (blessing) and Ifeanyicukwu (God is almightly).

The guests suggest their own names too, and before they go they will make donations and gifts of money. The grand-mother of the child is also given gifts. She is praised for the way she is looking after her daughter. The baby is handed to its mother. More wine is served before the party officially comes to an end. After all the visitors have gone, the host and hostesses go over all the names suggested and select one of them, which becomes the name of the baby.

1 3 *Oaths*

Every village in Iboland has a shrine where important sacri-fices are offered and where village festivities are celebrated. In charge of each shrine is a juju priest, often known as the chief priest. In addition there are private shrines and oracles. There are various uses of these shrines and oracles, but by far the most extensive use of them is in the administration of oaths.

Modern courts of law may err at times in the dispensation of justice but cases and disputes settled with oaths are im-partial. If two people have a dispute they go to the village council. The council always settles minor disputes and sends major ones to the village's chief priest. Such disputes often concern ownership of lands and trees. The chief priest offers libation in order to find out which shrine in the village is the most powerful at that particular time. The plaintiff and the defendant are given a list of things to buy. The first item in the list is either a white fowl or a white ram, depending on the severity of the dispute. Cohise chalk, wine, alligator pepper and azu-nkisi (a type of fish), follow their proper order in the list.

They are given a date. On that day, both of them report to the chief priest with their purchases. He prays to the gods and implores their help and guidance. Libation is poured and incantations used. He administers the oath to both of them. Whichever of them comes forward to claim ownership of the article or property in question, becomes the rightful owner. The procedure is that the person stands at the centre of a circle drawn with cohise chalk and says:

'Mighty and important god, I implore you to bear me witness that I am fighting for my rightful property. If I am struggling to take what does not belong to me, may I never live to see the sky any longer.'

Hardly has he finished speaking to the god when the juju priest declares the property in dispute his.

No person has ever been known to have told lies to a god. The penalty for taking a false oath is instant death. The defendant and plaintiff shake hands and walk away as friends. If a villager has threatened another villager with death, the juju priest takes a sample of blood from their thumbs. He mixes the blood and smears two pieces of kola nut with it. The men share the pieces of kola together. A few drops of the blood are put into a glass filled with palm wine; both of them drink from this glass, after which they shake hands. Each in turn goes to the altar and says:

'God of all gods, if ever the idea of killing a fellow villager crosses my mind again, you are free to mete out any suitable punishment to me.'

The advantage of this oath is that after its administration neither of the two men will commit murder in future.

At times Christians bring confusion with their religion, which is always looked upon with disdain. Instead of swearing by the gods, they prefer to use the Holy Bible. Unless the dispute is a trivial one, the Bible is never accepted by the village council.

14 *Palm fronds*

In most parts of the world a red piece of cloth flying on anything is indicative of danger. In Iboland, palm fronds indicate danger. Any compound or farm that is out of bounds is ringed round with palm fronds called igu or omu, in Ibo language. Trespassers go away as soon as they find the fence. It is an offence for someone to enter a farm that does not belong to him but it is a double one if the offender ignores the palm frond fence.

Lorries and vans carrying coffins indicate this with a number of palm fronds tucked in at the two ends of the vehicle. The idea behind this is to warn the traffic police that the lorry is not carrying fare-paying passengers. Moreover, prospective passengers need not stop the lorry once the palm fronds are conspicuously displayed. Fruit-bearing trees are often decorated with omu. This practice scares any potential rogues. It is said that the fruits of a tree so decorated have been dedicated to the gods and only the owner may rightly use them.

15 *Public and private societies*

A man's social status is gauged by the number of titles he has. Another yard-stick of his attainments is the number of societies to which he belongs. These societies fall into two chief categories – public and private societies. Most of them are open to members of the public, however. Entry requirements vary. The most important qualifications concern age, financial standing and family background. A further classification is according to age-groups. Some are composed of teen-agers, others of men of twenty to thirty years of age and others of men of over thirty.

A detailed study of all the societies – both the public and private ones – is likely to lead to ugly incidents since the activities of some are shrouded with secrecy. By far the most secret and worthy of study, are those organized by the 'grown-ups'. One of such societies is the masquerade cult. Here too, there are many variations. In Arondizuogu, for instance, the Ojionu is the most popular. In Akokwa, the Ogbamgbada is in vogue. In Aguata, the Achikwu predominates.

The Achikwu operates only during the night. Women and men of under thirty years are denied membership. Any man of thirty or over is free to become a member. He is enrolled into the cult and told when to come for the initiation ceremony. At the ceremony all the new members take an oath to keep the secrets of the cult. They attend a series of dancing practices designed to introduce them into the world of spirits and the occult. The house where practices are held is fenced with omu (palm fronds). Intruders are, therefore, warned.

After six months of strenuous practice, the cult decides to display to a limited number of members of the public. Such displays take place when a prominent villager dies, or during the annual village feast. At about ten o'clock, the chief medicine-man of the cult runs to the display ground. He stops at different places and pierces the ground with his Uji – a long rod shaped in the form of candlesticks – and then continues his journey. This is necessary in order to remove or render harmless, any 'medicine' that may be buried by a rival masquerade cult. He does not talk because a six-inch stick extends across his mouth. His presence on the roads is made known by the mysterious noise that accompanies his every step. Any person who hears the noise takes a different route or hides somewhere. Once satisfied that there is no danger, the medicine-man goes back to report to his cult. The beating of metal gongs heralds the arrival of the masqueraders. Women and children are never allowed to come and watch. The ground begins to shake as the masqueraders trot majestically to the display ground. Here the spectators have all gathered. Members of the cult call the masquers by their cult names as an honour, but spectators are not allowed to use these names. If any spectator uses these names, he has a very large fine to pay. All the livestock in the village are killed and he has to pay for them. The display continues until dawn.

23

Masquers

24

16 Teething

The teething period marks an important phase in the life of every child. The parents are the first to notice the appearance of the first milk teeth but they dare not tell anyone. Secrecy is essential. They keep their fingers crossed and wait for someone to announce the appearance of the teeth. Most people are aware of the responsibilities that devolve on whoever announces the child's teeth first. Some, on account of poverty, fail to say they have seen the milk teeth.

But as soon as someone notices the milk dentition, the parents jump for joy. They put on an air of affectation and open the child's mouth to see the teeth for themselves. Kola nut is brought and given to the discoverer. He may demand alligator pepper with his kola. Meanwhile, the child's father has sent a servant to buy one gallon of up-wine. After the drinking, the man goes home. He must have already told the host and hostess when next he is expected back. On this day tapioca is wetted and stewed and stockfish is kept handy. They await their guest's arrival with a remarkable amount of concern and anxiety.

As usual, the guest is confronted with kola and palm wine. The stewed tapioca crowns the entertainment. What he offers the child depends, by and large, on his social status. If he is an apprentice, not much is expected of him. The gifts given often include money, cosmetics, toys and always a fowl. The hostess jumps for joy and rushes out of the room to call the attention of the neighbours who are always inquisitive over such affairs. They are told what has happened and they too make their own presents. From that day onwards the child is fed with food adults take. Yam pounded and mixed with fresh palm oil forms the crux of his diet.

17 *The birth of twins*

The number of titles a man has and the number of societies
to which he belongs are all important pointers to his affluence.
The third important pointer is the number of children he has.
It is very unusual to find a man who is of age remaining single.
If he has no money to marry, friends and relatives may come
to his rescue. As soon as the right maiden is found the marriage
formalities are hurried over, and the two live together as
husband and wife.

The first two months are usually very embarrassing. The
husband is bombarded with questions such as:

'What is your wife like these days?'

'Any luck yet, man?'

'Are you sure your wife is not a man?'

'Do you ever sleep with your partner?'

All these questions have one thing in common. They are asked to find out if the wife is pregnant or not. If she is not, it is very
probable that both partners will start to worry. After the first
hundred market days (roughly a year), they go to a native
doctor or medicine-man for help. This doctor speaks to the village's ancestors and entreats them to help the young couple.

As soon as the wife becomes pregnant, the neighbours are
told and entertained lavishly. They all pray together, asking
the gods to give the host a male child. A family that starts
with a female child will have many obstacles to overcome in
future. Immediately the wife's labour is about to commence,
she is whisked off to a place where she will be given every
assistance she needs by a trained woman. The husband walks
up and down the house musing, and apparently having great
disturbing thoughts. He wonders what his fate will be if his
wife has twins.

The midwife runs away when she notices a second baby coming. She quickly looks for an egg which she breaks on the floor. Students of Ibo culture are not agreed as to what is the true significance of this action. The popular interpretation – and most people seem to favour this – is that the woman breaks the egg in order to free herself from the punishment that is imminent. She claims she has no part to play in the 'crime' and runs about the village sobbing. The village council meets and takes away the twins. These may be drowned or thrown into a mighty jungle where carnivorous animals abound. The mother is taken away to a place where mothers of twins are purified. Here she spends ten market days alone in her hut.

18 *Funeral of a titled man*

The illness of a titled man is made known to all the villagers. Top-ranking medicine-men are paid to look after him. If he has sons and daughters these are informed of their father's illness and they come home as quickly as possible. The ukoro, a large wooden call-drum, is sounded to tell the people that he has died. An interval of about ten minutes elapses before it is beaten again. The ukoro is reserved exclusively for announcing the death of prominent people, such as chiefs, warriors and titled men. The deceased's house is crowded by sympathizers. The body is washed and prepared for burial. The eldest son of the family, after consultation with other members of the family, announces the date of the funeral.

The chiefs of the neighbouring villages are also informed of the arrangement. The bereaved family expends a lot of

27

money preparing for the funeral. Cows, sheep, goats, bags of rice are bought and these may cost no less than a hundred pounds. The night preceding the great day, some housewives selected by the village council come to help. The animals are slaughtered by the men and the women go on with the cooking. At dawn, or even before the first cock-crow, guests from distant places start to arrive. The men carry their goatskins and drinking horns. Benches and chairs are borrowed from the village council and the area is fenced with palm fronds. These fronds help to ward off the heat of the sun. At eight in the morning the ceremony is opened by the chief or the oldest member of the community. Long speeches are given in praise of the deceased. Different types of kola nuts are served. A dozen young men serve the wine. Occasionally a song is started. Any sympathizer who has brought gifts hands these over to the widow or any of her children. Towards mid-day, food is served. Those living nearby may choose to go home and have their meals and come back in a few hours' time. The sympathizers from the neighbouring villages do not go away since they are all catered for.

It takes about three hours to clear the plates and dishes. Different societies and cults now display what they have been practising for a long time. Masquerades are shown and the masquers dance and entertain the spectators. Towards evening, an enlarged photograph of the deceased man is carried round the village. Sympathizers group themselves and sing while the procession continues. At dusk most of the sympathizers go, leaving behind those from far places. The bereaved family provides sleeping accommodation for them. Those who have friends and relatives nearby go to spend the night with them.

The distinguished villagers keep awake all night. The dangerous masquers now display. They are claimed to be using charms and can only operate at night. They are not seen but their presence is felt by the effect they have on the on-lookers. They disappear before the first cock-crow. Early in the morning the guests come back. The proceedings of the previous day are repeated. In the evening everyone goes home and the funeral ceremony ends with an address from whoever opened the function. The deceased is now said to be given a grand reception in the land of the dead.

19 *Worshipping of idols*

Every pagan has a shrine where he worships his gods. In all probability he must have inherited the shrine from his father. Early in the morning, before he goes to tap wine, he pays a visit to the shrine. With nzu (cohise chalk) he draws a circle round the shrine and stands at the centre of the ring. A piece of kola is brought which he chews and scatters all over the place. Next comes the alligator pepper. This also he chews and brings out. Squatting, he bids his god 'good-morning' and asks for his protection during the day. He goes away to continue his daily activities.

In the evening he comes back to the shrine. He repeats the same thing he did in the morning. This time he thanks his god for the protection given to him and his household and bids the god 'good-night'.

Women and children are not allowed to enter these shrines. There are special occasions when each pagan has to offer a special sacrifice to his god; also before harvesting the crops. There are other major occasions such as the village's annual

A juju priest offering a sacrifice to his god

festival, the outbreak of epidemics and a prolonged period of drought.

On each of these occasions he carries a gourd of palm wine. The traditional greeting over, he fills his drinking horn with wine and pours this on the ground. The horn is hit on the ground several times. He calls the god by his customary name: 'He who pays every man according to his merit.'

'The Saviour of mankind.'

'My Guardian and Protector.'

He is free to make up any names designed to give honour to the god. The god is told the problem facing the village and asked to help. Once in a while the worshipper comes to remove weed growing around the hut. If the elephant grass out of which the roof is fashioned is old, it is pulled down and a new one put in its place. Some pagans have their shrines near their homes. They are able to pay frequent visits to the gods if the shrines are near them. If a fowl is sacrificed to the god, the blood is sprinkled on the floor of the hut and on the statue of the god. The feathers are removed and left scattered while the meat is carried home. A pagan's day starts and ends with a visit to his god.

20 *Title taking*

A man's success in life is assessed by the number of titles he has. Wealth can make him famous but titles are always given priority. For one thing, a poor person can never afford to take a title – not even the smallest one. There are rigid rules which must be observed and the regulations are so many and rigorous that only the rich villagers can fulfil them. The qualifications vary according to the type of title wanted. In all cases, however, age and financial stability are taken into consideration. One point that needs mentioning is that there are a few titles which a man cannot take until his immediate elder brother has taken them.

If a villager wants a title he has to make a formal application to the red-cap chiefs. These chiefs are responsible for in-stalling new chiefs and initiating qualified men into different cults of importance. The council of chiefs meets and discusses the applicant's eligibility. If he satisfies the conditions laid down, he is strongly recommended and given a list of things he must buy. The sort of things he buys depends on the title he is taking. A basket of house-flies is often recommended in addition to other minor things of everyday use, viz, kola nuts, alligator pepper, home-made gin, cowries, clay pots, palm wine and stockfish. The red-cap chiefs fix the date as soon as they receive the requirements from the aspirant.

On the great day the aspirant puts on a leopard skin and prostrates himself on the altar. The red-cap chiefs are dressed in resplendent animal skins with feather-stuck red caps to match. Concoctions are prepared and libation poured. The oldest red-cap chief recites some incantations and pours a little of the concoctions on the prostrate man. Drinks are served. Each of the chiefs pats him on the cheek with a locally manufactured sword. He is now ordered to stand up and squat in front of the village's deity. He takes an oath promising to serve the village as best he can. A red cap is handed over to him and next a feather is added. One of the officiating chiefs gives him a fan and a sword. He is now a fully-fledged titled man.

A capping ceremony. A group of red-cap chiefs and titled men escort an aspirant to an altar for the capping ceremony.

The ceremony is now over and a procession of the chiefs takes place. The object of this ceremony is to put the new member on 'display' so that the villagers will know he has been received and accorded the status of a titled man.

21 *The new yam festival*

Sacrifices are offered to the gods before the land is cultivated. Immediately the year has run its course all the families busy themselves with clearing and burning in readiness for the planting season. Each family asks its own god to bless the farm and all the things that will be sown or planted. A few weeks later, the planting season starts. Yams are the concern of almost all the villagers. These will be ready for use towards the end of July.

Although they are available in the markets in July, no family thinks of eating these new yams until the end of the following month (August), or the beginning of September. A day is fixed for the new yam ceremony and the members of the family living in other villages are asked to return home for the 'big do'. This festival is not only used as a family reunion, but also as an opportunity to offer special sacrifices to the family's god or Chi, as it is commonly known. Laxative drugs are taken by all. New yams taken prior to the loosening of the bowels have a dangerous effect on the digestive system. Two or three cocks or even a ram, are purchased and slaughtered. If the family is a small one, one cock suffices. Before the family feast starts, the man of the family goes to his shrine to thank the god and give him his share of the food and meat.

The yams are cooked and served on oval dishes. All the members of the family sit around a table and all eat from the same dish. The meal over, the father cuts the meat and shares it among the members. If a cock is used, the head must be given to the youngest member of the family. The liver and the '*Ekoafo*' or gizzard, belong to the father and the hip goes to the first daughter. This occasion is strictly personal and this explains why guests are never invited. The family rises and says a prayer of thanks for staying alive to partake of the new yam festival. From that day everyone is free to eat the new yams whenever he chooses.

2 2 *Greetings*

As was pointed out earlier in this book, tradition has a very strong hold on the average Ibo: and one of the important traditions is that people should greet their elders. The distinguished personalities, such as chiefs and titled men, have their own peculiar greeting names. It is easier to greet a titled man than an ordinary villager. Take a titled man as an illustration. He may have chosen the name Epuechi (If we live to see another day) as his distinguishing name. Any villager seeing him any time during the day simply calls him by his distinguishing name, Epuechi. If the titled man does anything for him, the latter to express his appreciation, again says Epuechi. Titled men and chiefs are always called by their distinguishing names irrespective of the occasion. This contrasts oddly with the Western style of saying 'Good morning, good-afternoon/day, good evening, good-night and thank you'.

Ordinary folks are greeted in the same way as 'Westerners'. The difference is that the greetings are in the Ibo Language. Thus 'Isanachi' ('Good morning') and 'Kachifo' ('Good-night'). These traditional greetings are so much valued that any girl who fails to greet her elders will find it difficult to get a husband. The same problem faces a boy. If the offender is an adult he will probably be reported to the village council and he may lose some of the privileges to which he is entitled. Elderly women are addressed as Ndenne (Mother, worthy of reverence).

23 *Farm work*

The Ibos are chiefly farmers. In fact, an average family in Iboland does not buy food in the market. It uses what is obtainable in the family farms and gardens: yams, coco-yams, vegetables, pepper, tomatoes, cassava, etc. There is no doubt that a lot of hard work will have to be put in in order to obtain these innumerable commodities. For this reason communal or team work is always practised and encouraged. A family that has a large farm to till and cultivate, normally asks friends of the family to come and help. Farm implements – hoes, knives, sickles and shovels – are borrowed from neighbours and farming organizations.

As early as 4 a.m. on the arranged day, the wife of the owner of the farm starts preparing food to be carried to the farm. Foo-foo is pounded and a very tasty soup made. Tapioca is wetted and coconut is added. Fruits are also included and to crown them all, two of three gourds of palm wine are brought. At 6 a.m., the party sets out. A distance of, say, four miles may have to be covered. On arrival, the owner of the farm stoops down and takes sand from the ground. He moves a little and throws the sand up. This is necessary to render ineffective any poison left by an enemy. A common prayer is said and the work commences. All start from one spot and work towards the same direction. Now and then a joke is cracked and everyone laughs but this does not prevent the workers from going on. As soon as the sun appears in the sky they put down their implements and sit under a huge tree. It is time for breakfast. The food is washed down with palm wine and the work starts once again.

Towards evening the youngest members of the group are told to go and collect firewood. When the sun begins to set the work is suspended. If the work is not finished, another day is fixed. Each of the workers in turn invites the others to come and help him with his farm. At harvesting time each farmer sends some of the crops to all those people who helped him earlier in the year.

24 Wrestling

Throughout Iboland wrestling is an important sport. Young men have the chance to distinguish themselves and show their prowess. At times, disputes are settled with this all-important sport. An extremely popular girl who has had several approaches from suitors, may find it difficult to choose the man she will marry. What happens in this case, therefore, is that a wrestling competition is arranged for all the suitors and whoever emerges victorious marries the girl.

Inter-village wrestling competitions are not uncommon. Each village has its own wrestling ground, which is very soft and well looked after. The wrestlers are grouped according to their records of achievements. All the villagers are informed of any competitions, which usually come off in the evenings. A ring is made and spectators sit around this ring. The chief and titled men, the boys providing the music and the wrestlers sit inside the ring. Music is provided by boys who have been trained to produce this brand of music. The wrestlers squat and chat together. The competition is started by the two principal wrestlers from the two villages. Various techniques are employed and a wrestler can easily win the applause of the spectators with his adroit styles. Any competitor that is carried up – if his legs are no longer touching the ground – is declared defeated. Occasionally one competitor may be carried high up and thrown to the ground.

If it appears that no competitor is defeating the other, the wrestlers are said to be evenly matched. Another set of wrestlers comes in. Meanwhile, the boys are giving heart-stirring music, music that is capable of giving added strength to the weak. The total successes and failures of each team go to determine the result of the competition. The team that has the greatest number of successes becomes the winner and the chief presents the prize, which can take any form.

2 5 *Hospitality*

Visitors and strangers are often astonished by the way Ibos receive them. This way of life is inherited from their ancestors who hold that the gods can only help the villages if the villagers themselves are kind and open-hearted.

Neighbours come together in the evenings to chat. If any family has any wine to spare it informs the neighbours who come and drink. Women are even more hospitable than the men. Each housewife who prepares new soup sends a spoonful or two to the housewives living nearby. She asks them to tell her whether or not there is enough salt in the soup, or if there is too much pepper.

On important occasions every family sends food to the neighbouring families. If a family has a visitor the neighbours will all entertain the visitor in turn. The wife goes to the house where the visitor is lodging and asks the host or hostess to bring the visitor to her house. Secretly she will find out what the new-comer likes and then prepares that food. When the guests arrive, kola is served and food is brought. As always, palm wine is used to wash down the food. It is a sign of disrespect for the visitor to refuse the food. On the other hand, visitors are not supposed to finish all the food. They are expected to leave morsels of it. Otherwise the impression is created that the guest has not had enough food to eat for a long time. As a rule enough food is provided. Children who wash plates and dishes are unhappy if they do not find remnants of food on the plate or dish.

Part 2

Folklore

*A group of men, women and children sit in a
circle, tongue-tied, listening
to an elderly story-teller*

1 *Why women do not grow beards*

A long time ago women grew and wore beards. Theirs were longer and smoother than the men's. These beards were so long and curled that they served as purses.

There was a chief called Akim. Chief Akim was the most benevolent and competent ruler that had ever reigned. He treated all his subjects with due consideration and kindness and even went to the extent of distributing his wealth among the poor. This won him the admiration and love of all, rich and poor alike.

It had never been known for his army to be defeated. He had the strongest soldiers and he had the happiest subjects. The key to all his successes was an elephant tusk which he had inherited from his grandfather. This elephant tusk was preserved in a clayey dish which his pages took to the stream to wash daily. He valued his legacy so much that he had to remove the tusk himself every morning before giving the dish to the pages to wash.

One morning, however, he had a very important meeting with his advisers and forgot to remove the elephant tusk. The pages were not aware of this and took the dish and its content away to the stream. Just as they opened the lid, the tusk fell into the water. They swam and swam, searching for it, but their attempts proved unsuccessful. They went back sorrowfully and reported the loss to Chief Akim. The Chief sobbed and moaned.

'So I am powerless now,' he said. 'It's better for me to die instead of living as a woman. What am I without my protector?'

Chief Akim would have killed himself were it not for the prompt intervention of his advisers. A meeting of the Chief's advisers was held and it was decided to offer a reward of three hundred cowries to anyone who could recover the lost tusk. Fishermen and coin divers spent many nights searching for it. After six months every person gave up the search. It was not long before the Chief's kingdom was attacked and defeated by an enemy. Chief Akim was no longer as powerful as he used to be. On one occasion he was taken a captive, but was later released when a ransom was paid.

One cloudy morning a little boy went to the stream to fish. He was overjoyed when he found that he had caught a large fish, but to his surprise the fish spoke to him.

'Don't kill me, good little boy. If you will leave me in the water I shall reward you handsomely.'

Out of fear, the boy dropped the fish and moved a bit further away. He let go his hook and when he raised it he saw a long shining object attached to it. He was dazzled by the brightness of his find. He took it in his hand and started running home. On the way he was stopped by a young bearded woman.

'That's mine, boy; I lost it a week ago! I shall give you four sweets and one cube of sugar if you will give it back to me.'

The little boy gave away the tusk. On getting home, the thought of the day's incidents came back to him. He narrated the story to his father. The father and son went to Chief Akim. The Chief was extremely happy to hear that the tusk had been found. He was very anxious to have it back and he went to the woman's house. The woman said she was not in possession of the tusk. She further stated that she had been indoors all that day. A search was conducted; nothing was found. Her soup-pot was emptied and searched but again there was no tusk. They were about to leave her, when someone suggested:

'Examine her unkempt beard!'

The beard was searched and the elephant tusk was hidden there. Chief Akim pronounced a death sentence. The thief would be executed on the next market day, which was two days hence. Early in the morning the following day, the woman came to the Chief's house pleading for mercy. The Chief pardoned her but ordered that her beard should be brushed clean. An oil was applied to prevent any more growth of it. From that day onwards women ceased to grow beards. Chief Akim became powerful and popular again.

2 How the dog became a domestic animal

When the dog was living with his friends in the jungle he was a very wild animal – wilder than the lion. He flouted all the laws laid down by their king. All the animals were living together and men were living together too. These two societies were always at loggerheads with each other. The population of the animal kingdom was diminishing because men were hunting and killing their members.

Within the kingdom troubles were many and varied. Most of the complaints brought to the King were about the dog. There was nothing that could be done since the dog was about the strongest of them all. The chief of the human society summoned a meeting of his subjects and invited the King of the Animals to come. At the meeting, men promised to stop killing members of the animal kingdom but one condition had to be satisfied. They wanted the animals to give them one of

45

their members. All the animals were asked to attend a meeting convened by their King and were told what the men had said.

'Very good. Give them the dog,' some of them said.

'The dog – no-one else but the dog. Good riddance. Let him go to men now.'

There was a general uproar and the King was startled. He decided to put an end to the confusion by voting. The one hundred and five members present cast their votes. Eight of them wanted the fox to be given away, thirteen felt the antelope should be done away with, twenty-one wanted the lion to go, but the others said the dog must go. The dog was dismayed. He promised to turn over a new leaf, but the animals appeared stone-hearted. Men were asked to come and take away the dog.

The dog went with them and in a short time mastered the ways of living of his new neighbours. He threw away the crude ways of doing things. He had become a domestic animal.

A few months later there was a shortage of fish in the human society. The only solution to the acute shortage was to turn to meat, but there was no meat since the peace treaty was made between men and the animals. The remaining solution was to kill the dog, but this they would not do because he was a very useful member of their society.

'Let us break the peace treaty,' the chief adviser suggested.

There was no alternative but to implement the decision. Directed by the new member of the society, men killed many animals. The remaining animals were very uneasy. They felt the action was instigated by the dog. The King came to men to say he was ready to take back the dog and give another dozen animals in his place.

The dog refused to go.

'I am happy in my new environment,' he asserted.

The two societies have not come to terms to this day.

3 The peculiar shapes of the sun and the moon

The Sun and the Moon were once neighbours. They lived in harmony and shared most of their things together. The Moon was very beautiful and her charm and elegance impressed the Sun who was now developing love for her. When he could no longer keep quiet about his love, he approached the Moon and told her how he felt about her. The Moon simply chuckled and said nothing. Not discouraged, the Sun kept on struggling to win her affection. He showered her with gifts and did her manual work for her.

He spent one sleepless night thinking of how to propose to her. 'Suppose she refuses my offer, what shall I do?' This thought kept on coming to him. One evening he summoned all the courage he had and asked the Moon to marry him. To his surprise and delight, the Moon accepted his proposal. Twelve months after the marriage they had a daughter called Star. This girl was very beautiful, more beautiful than her mother. All their attempts to have more children failed. When Star was twenty-one her father wanted her to marry, but the Moon strongly opposed the idea. She had already planned that Star should remain in the family and rear up her own children within the household. By so doing she would help to increase the population of the family.

'You know you have no male child,' the Moon reminded her husband. 'Who will manage the affairs of the family when you die?'

'You'll die before me, my sweet wife,' the Sun gave her in answer.

This statement irritated the Moon. She picked up a broom

that lay on the floor and flogged her husband. The broom sticks stuck to the latter's face. The Sun in retaliation, picked up a sharp knife and cut his wife in two. Both of them separated leaving Star to own the house. Star later got married to a man of her choice.

This episode was responsible for the Sun and Moon's peculiar shape. The Sun appears today with little lines all around the face and the Moon often appears in two distinct halves.

4 Why hawks carry away chicks

In Sabo there was a married couple known as Eya and Oca. Oca was the wife of Eya. They were a happy pair and their visitors enjoyed spending a day or two with them. Despite the fact that they had married in their teens, they had not had a child. Old age was stepping in but they did not seem to bother until neighbours started tormenting them for their inability to have children. Eya did not pay attention to their tauntings which he regarded as empty talk which would vanish with time. Oca was a brave woman but often she spent nights crying and praying. She decided to go to a herbalist living near the market square. She had never known this man and the herbalist had never seen her before. But as soon as she entered the house, the herbalist addressed her by name.

'Good woman, Oca, welcome. You've done well by coming to see me. Our ancestors are with you and you'll become pregnant soon.'

The woman was astonished, she could not believe her ears.

Without making any comment she thanked the diviner and left the house. No sooner had she gone out than the man called after her. He advised her on the necessary steps to take in order to expedite the pregnancy.

Oca carried out these instructions and before long she became pregnant. She gave birth to a female child and she named the child Ada.

Ada grew up to be the most beautiful girl in Sabo. Before she was seven, as many as ten suitors had come asking her to marry them. The family's critics became admirers. Ada was adored by her parents who took good care of her. She was a dutiful and obedient child but she had one complaint – greed. She ate too much, but Eya and Oca did not consider this a problem since they had more than enough to eat.

When Ada was twelve, Eya and Oca wanted to go to their farm which was ten miles away. Food was prepared for Ada and a basket full of mangoes was brought out and left at her disposal; she was particularly fond of mangoes. She was strongly warned not to go to the mango tree that was at the back of the house.

As soon as her parents left, Ada ate all the fruits and gave her food away to the dogs. At midday she became hungry but could not get any food to eat. She went to the mango tree to pluck some mangoes.

An evil spirit was on one of the branches, resting.

'My wife, my wife,' it called out to Ada.

She looked around her but could not find anyone. Immediately she remembered that spirits used to come out at midday. She ran home. She did not tell her parents anything about the spirit when they returned in the evening. They were about to go to bed when a four-eyed spirit came in and wanted to take Ada away. Oca burst into tears. Eya offered money to the spirit but it refused to accept it. Oca reprimanded

49

C'

Ada for disobeying her, but it was no use! The spirit wanted nothing else except his wife, Ada. Oca took her daughter away and lectured her on how to escape from the new husband.

'Spirits always snore when they sleep,' she told her. 'When you find your husband snoring, stroke his chest lightly and draw out his tongue. If he does not wake up he is fast asleep, and that is the time for you to run away. But when you touch his tongue and he wakes up, tell him you are covering his mouth which he left open.'

Ada thanked her mother and went away with the spirit. She went to bed with it and was anxiously waiting for it to fall asleep. At certain times the spirit would wake up and find Ada still awake.

'Won't you sleep, wife? Don't you like my house?' he asked.

It was not long before the snoring began. Ada adroitly carried out the tests and finding them positive, crept out of bed and ran away. She had already covered two miles when she found out she was not taking the correct route. She saw an old woman who promised to send her home to her parents. She took Ada to her house and went out to confer with her friends. On looking aound, Ada saw fresh human heads dripping blood, and a number of skulls. She was petrified and dashed out in terror. The old woman, accompanied by her friends gave chase. Ada saw a hawk hovering over the sky and begged her to help. She sang:

> 'Sister Hawk come down and save me,
> Cannibals want to kill me.
> Sister Hawk make haste
> Or else I shall be dead.'

The Hawk came down and carried her away. It was already dawn when they arrived at Ada's house. Her parents were very glad to see her alive. They brought out a basket of yams and asked the hawk to accept it as a gift, but she refused. She said she wanted chicks. Oca brought out six chicks and put them in a little basket for her. With the aid of her beak the hawk carried the basket away. On the way, one of the chicks fell down. The hawk left it, saying she would come back to the earth and get it. She did not come till that year ended. When she came she found a hen with a dozen chicks, feeding.

'My chick must have grown and hatched out new chicks', she reasoned within her. She took one of the chicks away. At the end of that month she came and took another away. This is the reason why hawks carry away chicks.

5 *A moonlight song*

Our ancestors, we greet
   Goro – goro – dim – dim – goro
Your children are greeting
   Goro – goro – dim – dim – goro

What have you for us?
   Goro – goro – dim – dim – goro
Anything good for your children?
   Goro – goro – dim – dim – goro

Our fathers, are you there?
   Dim – dim – goro
What's heaven like?
   Dim – dim – goro

Prepare a place for us
   Goro – dim – dim – goro
We shall soon be there
   Goro – dim – dim – goro

Goro – goro – dim – dim – goro
Goro – dim – dim – goro
Dim – dim – goro
Dim – goro – goro – dim – goro

NOTE   This is a meaningless song. It is usually sung because of the effect it has on the people. Its music is accepted as an essential part of the enjoyment. The success of the song depends on how well the chorus is sung.

6 *A palm wine-tapper's song*

My little gourd is now full of wine
   Tinn – tinn – tinororo
Who is going to drink with me?
   Tinn – tinn – tinororo

My little gourd is now overflowing with wine
   Tinn – tinn – tinororo
My father-in-law is going to drink with me
   Tinn – tinn – tinororo

My little gourd is now full of wine
   Tinn – tinn – tinororo

Who is going to drink with me?
   Tinn – tinn – tinororo

My little gourd is now overflowing with wine
   Tinn – tinn – tinororo
Members of my family are going to drink with me
   Tinn – tinn – tinororo

Tinn – tinn – tinororo
Tinororo – tinororo
Tinn – tinn – tinororo
Tinororo – tinororo
Tinn – tinn – tinororo

7 *Intelligence squared*

The rat was going to see his sick grandfather one sunny afternoon, when he saw his one-time rival standing in front of his
house.

'Good day, Mr Tortoise, is that your house?'

The Tortoise replied:

'Hello, my learned friend, this is my house. Do please come
in for kola.'

The rat went in and the two friends and rivals sat down
together. The tortoise took French leave and went to his store.
He came back a few minutes later with a highly polished piece
of stone and offered it to the rat.

'This is kola, Mr Rat. Break it into pieces. I shall ask my wife to bring us alligator pepper.'

The rat looked at his host astonished. 'The same old trickster!' he told himself.

'Excuse me, Mr Tortoise, I want to go and ease myself. I shan't be long.'

He went out and came back with an old piece of cloth. He asked the tortoise to help him to lift up the ground.

'That's impossible,' exclaimed the tortoise.

The rat looked at him slyly and asked:

'Why on earth do you want me to break a stone for a kola nut?'

He stood up and went away to continue his journey. The tortoise asked him to call in again when coming home. After he had seen his grandfather, the rat called again on Mr Tortoise. The latter brought out a hen and a cock. He gave both of them to the rat asking him to bring back the hen whenever it started crowing, and the cock whenever it started laying eggs. The rat scratched his head and thanked the tortoise for his kindness. That night he killed the two fowls and made a tasty stew.

On the next market day he painted his face coal-black and rubbed his body with cohise chalk. He placed his hands on his head and ran to the market square shouting. People gathered to find out what was wrong; the tortoise too, was there.

'I received a message this morning that my mother was shot dead in the battle-field and my father died when he was about to give birth to a baby.'

The people looked at one another in amazement. They could not comprehend the joke, but the tortoise appreciated it. He went away dismayed.

8 *The tortoise and his father-in-law*

One day the tortoise wanted to find out if he was cleverer than his father-in-law. He called his wife and told her:

'See, I'm cleverer than your father. I wonder why people say your father is the father of tricksters and jesters.'

'You're still a child,' his wife told him. 'My father started his own tricks before any person was born.'

The tortoise fell down from where he was sitting. He laughed and laughed again at his wife's folly.

'Now tell me, who were the victims of your father's tricks since no person existed at the time he started his own tricks. You see why I say it's useless discussing things with women. You've contradicted yourself. Anyway, I believe in actions, not words.'

In the evening, the tortoise sent his son, Nwambe, to his father-in-law, Agadi, to tell him to buy him good palm wine. He was expecting some august visitors, he said. Nwambe went to Agadi and gave him the message. According to the tortoise's instructions, the wine should neither be locally produced nor imported. Agadi knew the type of son-in-law he had. A few minutes later he sent a messenger to him to say that the wine was ready. One condition attached, however, was that the wine should be carried by any person other than a male or female. This was above the tortoise's intelligence. He could not find an answer. After waiting in vain for his son-in-law, Agadi sent another messenger to tell the tortoise that anyone could carry the wine, provided such a person did not touch the gourd containing it. This condition was as difficult as, if not more difficult, than the first.

He called his wife and told her what her father had said. The wife laughed gaily and added:

'I told you my father is an experienced trickster. I don't expect you to compete with him in any way. What you ought to do is to ask him to teach you some of his tricks.'

The tortoise would never admit any failure. He told his wife that he was simply finding out what sort of father-in-law he had.

9 *The butcher's share*

There was a great famine in the land of the animals. This was caused by drought. All the animals were dying of starvation as a result.

Five rabbits were looking for food. They were not looking for something very delicious. No! They wanted anything that could help to fill empty stomachs. They came to a river bank and saw the carcass of a monkey. They gave praise to their ancestors and immediately set to work. They could not cut the meat because their claws were rather blunt. As they were thinking about what to do, an equally hungry lion passed by and stopped. He had seen what he had been looking for. The rabbits were happy to share the meat with him because he had long and sharp claws.

He divided the meat into six equal parts but all of a sudden he scattered the six portions and started afresh. He divided it into two equal parts. One part he reserved for himself and called it the 'butcher's share'. He shared the other half equally among them. The rabbits protested but kept quiet when he threatened to take all the meat. He left them and went to a nearby bush to get some leaves with which to wrap his own share. He was anxious to take the meat to his new wife as soon as he could make it. The rabbits hit on an expedient! They grouped themselves in threes and 'died'. The remaining two awaited the lion's arrival. When he came he was told that the other three rabbits were dead and that it was customary for them to die in groups of three.

'Come and complete our number so that we shall "die" together,' one of the rabbits suggested.

The lion looked around him in surprise.

'Me? Not me! I'm not ready to die yet. Remember, I've just married a new wife and, moreover. . .'

He took to his heels before he could finish his statement. The three rabbits rose up and quickly re-shared the meat amongst themselves.

10 *The tiger and the monkey*

The tiger had the misfortune of falling into a water reservoir. He screamed and asked for help but none came. This water reservoir was situated in an unfrequented region. It was then the harmattan season and the water reservoirs and wells were all dried up. The tiger was lucky. He could easily have been drowned if the reservoir had contained any water. He spent three days in this dungeon without any food or drink.

It was on the fourth day that help came. The monkey was passing along when he heard the faint scream of somebody — someone obviously in great distress. He went to the reservoir and saw the tiger worn out and almost dead. He stood near the edge of the reservoir and threw in his tail.

'Hold my tail,' he instructed the tiger.

This the tiger did and was brought to the surface. Instead of thanking the monkey he pounced on him ready to tear him to pieces. The monkey pleaded, but his assailant was not prepared to listen. The crow flew past the scene and noticed something wrong. He came down and asked the monkey what the matter was.

'I was having a stroll when I heard someone screaming. I came to find out who it was. It was the tiger; he was trapped in the reservoir. I gave him my tail to hold and rescued him, but instead of being grateful he said he would kill me.'

The tiger confirmed that the story was a true one.

'You surprise me, Mr Tiger. I always thought you were very considerate. Why this uncouth behaviour now?' the crow queried him.

'I don't want to offend the monkey but you see I have not had any food for the past four days. I shall die if I don't have something to eat before long.'

'I agree with you, Mr Tiger,' the crow stated. 'Why not express gratitude to your benefactor before you feast on him? If I were you that's exactly what I should do.'

The tiger wanted to know how best he could express his gratitude. He did not like the way the crow was delaying things.

'I'm getting very impatient, Mr Crow. Be fast, otherwise I shall die of starvation.'

The crow asked him to bend down near the reservoir and

raise up his fore limbs. The tiger in his attempts to do this fell back into the reservoir. He pleaded for help, but the monkey and the crow jeered at him.

He died the next day.

11 *The foolish goat*

A certain goat picked up a piece of yam
    Nzamiri
And wanted to cross a river
    Nzamiri

There was a plank for a bridge
    Nzamiri
And the goat stood on the bridge
    Nzamiri

He was fascinated by the river
    Nzamiri
It was the first he had ever seen
    Nzamiri

Looking into the water he saw an image
    Nzamiri
Little did he know it was his own image
    Nzamiri

He noticed the yam in the goat's mouth
    Nzamiri
He felt it was bigger than his
    Nzamiri

'I want that yam,' he said
       Nzamiri
'And I must get it,' he concluded
       Nzamiri

Nzamiri – zanza – nzanza
Nzamiri – zanza – zanza

S – sh – h s – sh – sh – sh – s – sh-hh
The water roared as he dived in
S – sh – h – s – sh – sh – sh – s – hh
The torrents thundered in anger.

The foolish goat was drowned
       Nzamiri
Greed caused his death
       Nzamiri

The lesson from the story
       Nzamiri
Is that we must be content
With what we have.
       Nzamiri

Nzamiri – zanza – nzanza
Nzamiri – zanza – zanza.

12 *Sharing the booty*

The hyena, the tortoise and the antelope were great friends.
Their friendship was such that the tortoise gave his daughter

in marriage to the antelope; the antelope gave his son as a servant to the hyena, and the hyena in turn, gave his daughter to help the tortoise's wife, who had a new child.

The threesome went on a hunting expedition. On the way they tracked down a lamb which they killed. The next animal to fall a victim was the owl. As they were resting under an iroko tree, a big zebra dashed past.

The three hunters gave chase. The zebra was overpowered and killed.

'Now friends, it's getting dark. Come, let's share our booty and go. By the way, how shall we share them? Any suggestions, comrades?' The hyena asked them.

The antelope gave an answer.

'You take the owl, the tortoise has the lamb and the zebra belongs to me. What do you say, Mr Tortoise?'

'Nonsense! Nonsense!' roared the irate hyena, 'what did you say, antelope?' He gave the antelope a good jab on the face, and the latter ran away to save himself from further punishment.

'Now that the foolish antelope has fled, how shall we share the booty, Mr Tortoise? It will be interesting to hear what you have to say.'

'That's the easiest job on earth,' replied the crafty tortoise.

'Tell me then,' the impatient hyena retorted.

'Well,' said the tortoise, after clearing his throat, 'you'll have the owl for your breakfast; the lamb for your dinner; and the zebra for your supper.'

'How wise you are, Mr Tortoise! Who has taught you all the wise things you know?'

The two friends set out for home. On arrival the tortoise went to the antelope, who was still nursing the injuries he had received from the hyena. They decided to severe their friendship with the hyena.

13 Mr All-of-You

A thousand years ago animals were classified into two major groups – those that could fly and those that could not. The two groups were friendly with each other and had a common meeting annually. In addition, the flying animals had a feast which was held annually in commemoration of their abode in the sky. That year's festival was to be held in the sky, and for this reason only the animals that could fly were invited. The tortoise was not happy with this arrangement, it had been his ambition to go. Therefore, he went to the animals that could fly and made his intention known to them.

'But that's impossible, Mr Tortoise, you can't fly,' one of them reminded him.

'I know I cannot fly and that's why I have come to you for help.'

He was asked to go home and come back the following day. When he left, the animals thought of ways to help him.

'Let us take him with us. He is the most renowned traveller among us and he is also well grounded in etiquette.' The woodpecker continued his speech: 'I suggest he comes along with us. I volunteer to bring him. I have a big bag which can accommodate him conveniently.'

This idea was praised but the pigeon had an even better plan.

'Let us all give him three feathers each. These feathers will be gummed together and he can fly like us.'

This plan was sanctioned and adopted. The tortoise was mad with excitement when he was told the following day that he could go with them. Two more days to go before the big feast. The tortoise told them not to take any food or drink on the day preceding the great day. It would be grossly unfair not to finish the food to be provided by their hosts and hostesses, the tortoise warned. In the evening he lectured them on how to behave on arrival.

'The animals of the sky want their guests to have names. You must all choose different names by which you will be known in the heavens.'

The heron chose the name Black Beauty; the weaver-bird chose the name Delegate and the crow chose Double-Beauty. All of them chose very beautiful names but the tortoise after due thought, said his was All-of-You.

On the day arranged they left together. The tortoise looked resplendent in his multi-coloured wings. He was a bit nervous and awkward because that was his first flight. The animals of the sky were pleased with their guests, particularly their keen sense of time. Formal greetings were exchanged and kola was served. A huge dish of rice was brought and placed on the central porch around which the guests sat.

'Who has the dish of rice?' the tortoise asked the steward.

'It is for all of you,' was the answer.

The tortoise addressed his companions: 'Friends, you see why I told you we should have names. The animals of the sky have a queer way of entertaining visitors. Each guest is served individually, and as you can see, the leader of the team is always served first.'

Meat was brought and as usual the tortoise finished it alone. He could not finish the wine brought and in order that no-one else should drink it, he washed his hands in it. The other animals were getting very impatient with their hosts and hostesses. To their surprise, someone came to announce that the party had officially come to an end.

'But we have not had any food as yet,' the hungry vulture told him.

It was soon clear that the tortoise had deceived them. In anger they removed their feathers from his body and flew home. He implored some of his friends to take him home, but they refused. At last, the wren consented to help.

'I want to help you, Mr Tortoise, but the trouble is – I cannot carry you.'

'I tell you one thing you can do for me. Tell my wife to bring pillows, rags and all the soft things in the house, outside, then I can fall down safely.'

The wren flew home but gave the tortoise's wife a different instruction. Axes, knives, hoes and all the various hard things in the house were piled up. The tortoise saw all this but could not discern whether they were hard or soft articles. He released his grip and fell down. He shattered his shell and was rushed to the soldier-ant, who stitched the pieces together.

This is the reason why the tortoise has several markings on his shell.

14 *The penalty of pride*

The squirrel had always been told that the reindeer was a very intelligent animal. Everyone seemed to be virtually in love with this animal because of her agility. The little squirrel's one ambition was to meet this animal called the reindeer and if possible to have a talk with her. She was going to visit her husband one morning when she met an unusual animal. It struck her that this might be the reindeer. She greeted her:

'Wise reindeer, I greet you.'

The animal turned back and responded. The squirrel knew instantly that this was the much talked-of animal. She decided to await her return in order to talk to her. A couple of hours later the reindeer came. Fright overtook the squirrel. She opened her mouth but no words came.

'How are you getting on these days with your husband?' the frightened squirrel managed to ask at last.

The reindeer looked at her disdainfully and walked away. Then she changed her mind and came back to address her questioner.

'You little creature, aren't you afraid to speak to me? Your parents could not speak to me and now that they are dead, you think you'll do what they failed to achieve. How do you know I'm married? Now tell me, you haughty, squinting creature, how many tricks do you know?'

'Only one, wise reindeer.'

The reindeer laughed and asked the squirrel to tell her which trick she knew.

'I know I have to climb a tall tree as soon as I see an elephant.'

The reindeer laughed again and asked the squirrel to follow her to a cliff where she would teach her more tricks. The latter could not believe the reindeer. Hardly had they sat down to discourse, when two elephants galloped by. The squirrel quickly climbed a tree and watched the three animals. The reindeer could not effect an escape. She was trampled to death by the elephants.

'Save yourself with your many tricks,' the squirrel called out, unaware of the reindeer's death.

15 *The tortoise trapped*

A great famine ravaged the earth. At least ten animals died daily. Those animals that were fortunate enough to go on living were reduced to mere skeletons. Only one animal appeared to be unaffected by the scarcity of food. The bull was the lone exception. He had a hut in a forest where he usually had his three daily meals. Each time he arrived at the hut he said some incantations and whatever food he wanted appeared. The tortoise was quick to notice that the bull was getting fatter and fatter each day. One morning he paid him a visit and wanted to know what kept him so fresh and robust. The bull told him.

'I'm almost dead, Mr Bull, can you please take me with you this afternoon? I am asking for one meal only, not two.'

'No thank you. You're known throughout the land for your cunning and treachery.'

'That's true,' replied the hungry tortoise, 'but I am glad to tell you that I have turned over a new leaf a long time ago. Remember our ancestors saying that "a friend in need is a friend indeed". Kindly help me.'

The bull was moved and asked the tortoise to come back in the afternoon. He came back in the afternoon with an old leather bag filled with ashes. As they were going, he made a tiny opening in the bag and the ashes marked the bush pathway they took. On arrival, the bull recited some words and the hut was replenished with different types of food. The usually insatiable tortoise was satisfied.

In the evening, he decided to have his supper alone in the magic hut. He found his way very easily by following the marks left by the ashes he carried in the afternoon. When he reached the hut he said the very words the bull had used earlier in the day. Food came out and he ate to his satisfaction. He wanted to carry all of it home, so he continued saying the magic words. The walls of the hut collapsed and he was trapped. It was not long before the bull came to have his supper. He saw the tortoise trapped. In his anger, he took a club and broke all the bones in the hands and legs of the glutton. He then set him free, but from that day onwards, the tortoise has not been able to walk fast.

16 *A fight of wits*

There was an annual feast in the animal kingdom. This was held to celebrate the gathering in of the harvest. All the distinguished personalities were invited and the tortoise was one of these. Uninvited guests were not allowed, but each guest was allowed to bring his servant or a member of his family with him. Drinking horns and calabashes for serving food and kola were brought by each one invited. Another characteristic of this annual Kensi (for this was the name of the feast) was that no guest was allowed to carry meat home unless he had a servant. The feast was drawing near but the tortoise had not, as yet, got a servant to go with him.

He approached Mrs Sheep and asked her permission to take her youngest son, Faye, with him. Mrs Sheep asked Faye to follow him. On the way, the tortoise dropped his drinking horn and showed his servant the place where he had left it. A few yards further on he left the calabashes. They were some minutes late and took their seats near the chairman's table.

Kola nuts were served. He asked Faye to run and bring one of the calabashes. Meanwhile, he'd borrowed one from a fellow-guest. When the servant came back he reprimanded him seriously for coming back late.

'What have you been doing on the way?' he said.

Faye was sent to bring the remaining calabashes when food was brought. The tables were being cleared when he came back.

'You're late again. What's wrong with you?' the master interrogated the servant.

Palm wine was served and as usual, Faye went to get the drinking horns, only to find on arrival that he had missed the drinks too. Every guest was happy and satisfied except Faye. The tortoise wanted to cover his monstrous deed. He mixed palm oil and warm water and forced Faye to drink. His stomach protruded after this drink. To crown it all, the tortoise forced a nut into his servant's rectum. Mrs Sheep was happy to see how well fed her son was.

'The poor thing must have overfed himself,' she concluded to herself. 'Go and bring me the red mat on the kitchen ceiling,' she commanded the worn out Faye.

As he climbed to bring the mat, Mrs Sheep noticed the kernal stick in his rectum. She forced it out and instantly the mixture of oil and water flowed out, and Faye fell down stone dead! Mrs Sheep burst into tears, but there was nothing else she could do.

The following year important guests were invited to attend the Kensi. The tortoise was on the priority list. He went to Mrs Sheep to take one of her sons with him. Mrs Sheep bluntly refused to give him any of them. The eldest son, Hasa, volunteered to go with him. His mother refused to give him her permission, but when she became tired of Hasa's incessant pleadings, she reluctantly allowed him to accompany the tortoise. Hasa was different from Mrs Sheep's other sons. He could fly like a bird and was highly intelligent.

On the day of the Kensi they set out on their way. The crafty tortoise dropped his drinking horn, which he showed to his servant and companion. As soon as he continued his journey, Hasa flew quickly and brought the horn. He then put it in a bag which he carried with him. The tortoise did not know that his companion had a bag with him, neither did he know that he could fly. He dropped the calabashes and Hasa picked them up. When they arrived at the place he sent Hasa to bring a calabash for kola. In the twinkling of an eye he came back with a calabash. The tortoise was not happy and refused to take the kola. Food was served. The servant wasted no time in bringing the remaining calabashes.

'You're a greedy child! Do you want to break your legs and hold me responsible?'

He refused to share the food with Hasa. The boy finished the meal alone. The same thing happened when drinks were served. The tortoise had not tasted anything yet but was buried in deep thought. There was a woman selling food at the back of the building where they were. The woman was not expected to see any of her customers. The tortoise gave her twelve cowrie shells and asked her to prepare soup for him. He wanted *alibo* and *ogbono* soup made out of yam and mango seeds. He said he would come and have the food at seven o'clock in the evening. Hasa knew of this intrigue. He went back to the woman and disguised himself as the tortoise. He complained of a little dizziness and urged the woman to prepare his meal for six o'clock instead of seven.

'I hope I've paid you?' he asked the woman.

'Have you forgotten? You have paid me my twelve cowrie shells.'

As soon as the sun set, Hasa knew it was six o'clock and

went to have his meal. At seven the tortoise went for his meal. The woman shouted and accused him of theft. The tortoise escaped with little injuries inflicted on him by the turbulent mob of angry animals. The Kensi was now declared closed. Each guest was given meat to take home. The tortoise did not want to share it with his equally-crafty servant.

'We shall sleep here because it is already dark. Very early tomorrow morning we'll go back.'

The servant praised his master's suggestion. At midnight the tortoise carried the meat in a rectangular basket and went home. Hasa saw him and flew fast to meet him. He perched on the basket the master was carrying and devoured all the meat leaving only the bones. To make up for the loss in weight he picked little pebbles and added to the bones.

The tortoise called on his wife to prepare soup. He had brought meat to last them a fortnight, the tortoise told her. At dawn the wife came to take some meat for the soup. To her surprise, she saw pebbles instead of the meat, and resting at a corner of the rectangular basket was Hasa. She raised an alarm. When the tortoise came, Hasa left the basket and perched on the head of Afoefu, the only child of the tortoise.

'Don't shake your head, Afoefu,' he instructed his son.

He picked up a knife and threw it at Hasa. Afoefu shook his head and his head was chopped off.

Hasa was happy that he had at last avenged his brother's death.

17 *Mr Ostrich catches a thief*

The ostrich was a very popular animal. His foresight and industry endeared him to all his friends. It was said he had the biggest plantation throughout the land. Some of his friends went to his plantation at night to steal his fruits; he knew of this and walled his plantation. To secure his fruits further, he left no gates except a small circular opening which he left at the rear end of the plantation. There was no day that he did not pay a visit to the farm.

One cloudy market day, the lizard and the rat stole into the farm. They found piles of palm fruits heaped by the walls. It goes without saying that they started to eat the fruits.

'Keta – keta – keta – keta,' their mouths produced rhythmic music.

Now and then the lizard went out of the farm to come back a few minutes later.

'What is wrong, my friend?' the worried rat wanted to know.

'Nothing, mate. I went to clean my oily mouth on the walls.'

'I see.'

This continued. The lizard went out of the plantation several times.

'Hush! hush! What's that noise I hear?' the lizard drew the attention of his companion.

'Isn't today the market day? It's not very likely . . . '

Before the rat could finish his speech, the owner of the farm was at the entrance. Both friends ran round the plantation. The lizard went out through the circular opening. He had often gone out of the opening to make sure his stomach was not getting bigger than the opening. The rat had no such idea. He found he could not escape through the opening. The ostrich caught him and gave him a thorough beating.

18 *The big test*

There were many reports of murder coming to Chief Nkapi, the chief and ruler of all the animals. A new law was made that no animal had the right to kill another animal. Offenders would be punished by hanging them in the market square. The little and weak animals were particularly delighted. Before this legislation, carnivorous animals, such as the lion and the tiger, could and did kill little innocent ones.

The pig had a wife whom he loved very much. They met when they were working for Chief Nkapi. After a brief period of courtship they decided to get married. One day the pig wanted to test the wife. He had been telling her all his secrets and now he wanted to find out how really secret those secrets were. He went to the back of his house and dug a pit. He then covered it, and sobbing and panting, went to his wife.

'I was fighting with the duck when I lost my temper and gave him a blow on the head. He fell down and died, and I've just buried him at the back of the house.'

'Oh dear!' the wife exclaimed. 'Come and show me where you buried him.'

The pig showed her the spot.

'Don't worry, my husband, as long as you don't tell anyone else, no-one will hear of it.'

Two days later the duck was reported missing. A search party was organized to look for him, but his whereabouts could not be traced. He had gone to a distant village to marry a wife. He had told no-one of his plans except the pig, and that was why the pig said he'd killed the duck.

On the next market day, the pig and his wife fought. The wife went to the Chief's palace to announce the death of the duck. The Chief, accompanied by six of his courtiers, came to the pig's house where the wife pointed at the spot of burial. The pig was bundled-off to the Chief's cell. When he saw that he would be killed, he told Chief Nkapi that he had not killed the duck.

The Chief did not appear to believe him. He ordered that the duck's body should be exhumed. The men dug the ground, but nothing was seen. The pig was still held a prisoner. He spent many days without food. He called Chief Nkapi and narrated the story. Still the Chief doubted the veracity of the story. The pig therefore took them to Alamo, where the duck was. There, they saw the duck enjoying his honeymoon with his new wife. The pig was set free and the Chief rewarded him for the unjust punishment he had received.

On arrival home the first thing the pig did was to send away his wife.

'You have failed the big test,' he told her.

19 *The dove and the woodpecker*

The dove and the woodpecker were good friends. The one lived in the sky while the other lived on the earth. The dove was still a bachelor and he paid frequent visits to the woodpecker and his wife. Each time he called on the couple he was given food, and when he was ready to go they gave him food to take with him. The woodpecker advised his wife to entertain the dove well, whether he (the woodpecker) was in or not. One day the dove came as before. He was given bread-fruit and sweetened tapioca. Rice was parcelled for him to take home.

'I shall pay you a visit tomorrow,' the woodpecker informed his friend.

The latter fell a-laughing.

'Mind you, you cannot fly. I still live in the sky!'

The woodpecker was not happy with his friend's remark. The dove promised to give his friend a gift worth over thirty cowrie shells, if ever he managed to come to his abode in the sky.

The next morning the woodpecker told his wife to wrap him up with five cups of rice and give the parcel to the dove.

'If he asks about me, tell him I've gone to see my in-laws, living twenty-four miles away.'

He was wrapped up with the rice. The dove was given food to eat when he came and the made-up parcel was given to him when he was ready to go. He thanked the hostess and went away.

'I wonder what is in this parcel – it is very heavy.'

However, the dove did not give any more thought to the parcel. He left it in one corner of the kitchen when he reached home. The woodpecker tore open one end of the parcel and came out. He went to his friend's hut where he found him resting. The dove was amazed to see him.

'How did you manage?' he asked the intruder. He went to his kitchen and saw the parcel torn. 'What a dishonest friend you are! So you've been doing this dirty business for a long time now? No wonder I lost my soup five days ago!'

In fury he threw the woodpecker down to the earth. Ever since then, the dove and the woodpecker have been bitter enemies.

20 *An unforgettable day*

Mr Green-turtle woke up one morning feeling on top of the world. There was nothing unusual that particular day and only the green-turtle knew what had caused his exhilaration and ecstacy. After taking his breakfast he dressed up and went to the pathway leading to the village's stream. Here he sat down on a baobab tree. An old magpie came. She was very old and moved with great difficulty. The green-turtle started to laugh when he noticed this unusual gait.

The green-turtle's attitude annoyed the magpie. She invoked the spirits of her ancestors to punish the saucy green-turtle. She stooped down and collected sand from the ground and then threw it on him.

'I promise you the trouble you're looking for. You will soon meet someone who is as troublesome as you are.'

'I want trouble and the sooner I get it the better. Nothing save trouble will satisfy me,' the green-turtle gave in reply.

The moth was going towards the stream when the trouble-seeker saw him. He took away the fish he was carrying. The moth went and reported the incident to their Chief. The Chief felt the moth must have been at fault. He sent the wasp.

'Carry this dish containing fish to my worker near Ara stream,' he instructed the wasp.

On the way the green-turtle intercepted the wasp and ate the fish. The bee was sent and the same thing happened. The Chief sent some of his intelligent subjects to go and lure the green-turtle to his palace. When the offender arrived he was given a tumultuous reception. The Chief ordered food to be given to him. This food contained poison. He was asked to go home and come back to the palace the next day.

At home he called a few of his friends and narrated the

story. He did not want to go back to the palace, but he knew the Chief had given him something that could make him change his mind. At dawn his friends covered him with a heavy mortar. As soon as the green-turtle heard the drumming from the Chief's palace, he overturned the mortar and went to the palace.

He was arrested and tied to a tree.

'At midday you'll be killed,' the Chief told him.

He was left alone. The Chief and his subjects continued their normal daily activities. The green-turtle saw the old magpie he had insulted the previous day, and appealed to her for help.

'Serves you right, you've seen the trouble you've been looking for.'

The magpie went away. The leopard saw him and pitied him. He stood on the green-turtle and squeezed out all the food he'd taken for the past three days. The poison came out with the food and he ran home.

He threw a lavish party for all his friends.

'I will not look for trouble any more,' he assured his guests.

21 *Slow and steady wins the race*

There was once a dispute among the animals regarding the fastest runner amongst them. The hare was proud and claimed superiority because of his agility. Surprisingly enough, the tortoise claimed that he was the fastest. His own speed – according to him – was inherited from his grandfather. Other animals traced their agility to their great, great-grandfathers. It was not long before the animals withdrew their statements leaving the hare and the tortoise to vie for the honour. Most animals asked the tortoise to withdraw his statement, but he remained defiant.

'I am a man of actions; not words. Let's have a running contest, the hare and I, and we shall prove our talents.'

His suggestion was praised and they were asked to cover a distance of five miles. The lion, tiger, leopard and fox were asked to go to the market five miles away and wait for the two competitors. The tortoise and the hare started from the same place. The other animals watched excitedly to see what hope the slow tortoise had. Each step he took measured one quarter of an inch, whereas his rival's measured five and a half feet. The hare covered a distance of two miles and turned back.

When he arrived at the starting point he was cheered by his admirers. He started the race again and soon overtook the tortoise on the way. He stopped at the three-mile corner to take a little snuff, after which he decided to take a few minutes' rest before continuing the race. He soon fell asleep.

As soon as he woke up he continued. He neither stopped on the way nor looked sideways. If he suspected any obstacle on his way, he collected his whole strength and gave himself a throw. He did not meet the tortoise on the way and he concluded he had jumped over him thinking he was a tree stump.

He was booed by almost all the animals when he finished the race. To his surprise he saw the tortoise being led in triumph by the animals.

'What did I tell you, friends?' the victor asked rather stoically. 'I inherited my speed from my grandfather.'

The tortoise and the hare lined-up for a race

22 The fruit of labour

The dry season was the period when all the insects worked hard on their farms, preparing for the rainy season. During the rainy season they all remained indoors eating what they had stored during the dry season. It was now dry season, and the insects were toiling hard on their farms replenishing their barns.

The locust and the praying mantis were friends. The praying mantis was a happy-go-lucky insect and always sang while his friend worked. The locust advised him to go and gather grain in his own barn in readiness for the rainy season.

'It's no matter, there is still plenty of time,' the lazy mantis replied.

At times he related stories to the locust, who was not interested. Several times he warned him to go and prepare himself for the change of weather. The mantis was no longer happy staying with his friend. He went to the bee. As usual he danced and sang while the busy bee overworked himself. The bee occasionally brought food and wine which they shared together.

The mantis became ill and could no longer sing and dance. For eight market days he could not leave his house. As soon as he became well again he started his merry-making.

'Why not go and do a little work on your farm, now that you are well again?' the bee suggested.

'Next week. I shall start next week.'

The rainy season came earlier than expected. Every one was surprised but the insects were not worried since they had been storing grain for use during the wet and rainy days. But the praying mantis was worried. He had already used all the grain he had when he was ill. He went to the locust to borrow some.

'Go to your new friend, the bee,' was the locust's answer.

He went to the bee but the latter was not prepared to help. The third week of the rainy season saw the praying mantis dead.

23 *A sumptuous meal*

Mr Tortoise had a palm plantation. Most animals had their plantations as well. He spent the greater part of his time weeding and tending the palm trees. He was meticulous about the dividends which the plantation yielded. One day he went to fell some ripe fruits. One palm fruit fell down and he decided to pick it up in case a fowl should carry it away. By the time he had come down, the fruit had already gone down a ravine. The tortoise went down the ravine as well.

'I must never leave this fruit,' he assured himself.

The ravine led him to an unknown land where he met several spirits. He was warmly received and taken to the Prince of the Spirits. He was trembling with fear when he saw the Prince.

'We've taken your fruit, but we shall reward you if you will sleep here. Tomorrow morning we shall compensate you for the lost fruit.'

The tortoise was impressed by the Prince's speech. At night he was given two beds – a new bed with drawings on it, and an old one with dirty boards. He chose the old one. The spirits were touched by his humility, and he was given the new bed instead.

When he wanted to go home the following morning, he was

presented with two drums – one old and one new – and asked to take one. Again he chose the old one. He was told how to beat the drum in order to get food. This drum produced all sorts of food, ranging from foo-foo to rice and beans.

On getting home he locked himself in a room and beat the drum. Food came out and he ate and had enough. The next day he invited all the animals. Some were contemptuous of the tortoise's invitation; others, accepted the invitation in good faith. He placed a hollow dish in front of each guest and closed all the doors and windows. The drum was beaten and different types of food were obtained. Each guest chose the type he wanted. They all sang in praise of the host and thanked him for his magnanimity.

As a sign of appreciation they conferred a chieftaincy title on him. When the story of Chief Tortoise's kindness was told, the disobedient animals blamed themselves for not going. It was too late because the magic drum was already exhausted.

A few days later, Chief Tortoise went to fell some fruits in his plantation. As he did so he wished a fruit would fall into the ravine where the one had fallen a couple of days ago. None fell and he came down and pushed one into the ravine. Very soon he arrived at the land of the Spirits, who knew what trick he had planned. At night he was given an old bed to sleep on. Very early in the morning he said he was going home. Two drums were given to him – one old and one new. He chose the new one.

'If an old drum can produce so much food' he argued within himself, 'the new one will no doubt treble the food production.' On getting home, he locked himself up and beat the drum. To his dismay, three monsters jumped out and would have flogged the life out of him had he not deserted the room.

'He who shares in merry-making, also shares in suffering.'

With this maxim in mind he summoned all the animals. This time every animal turned up. Chief Tortoise appointed the elephant to serve the food. He locked all the doors and windows and then took permission and went away.

The drum was struck and six ugly looking monsters came out. The animals were beaten mercilessly. There was a stampede but no exit. In the mad confusion that followed, some small and weak animals were killed.

24 *Eight Commandments for children*

Little children love your mother
    Akpakoro – kpankoro
Fear your father and obey your seniors
    Akpakoro – kpankoro

Little children, love your mates
    Akpakoro – kpankoro
For that's the origin or real love
    Akpakoro –kpankoro

Children, children, say your prayers
    Udumo – ogene
Ask Him to teach you to be chaste
    Udumo – ogene

Children play when it's time to play
    Udumo – ogene
Children work when it's time to work
    Udumo – ogene

Children, do you know what to avoid?
   Akpakoro – kpankoro
Do you know what you mustn't tell anyone?
   Akpakoro – kpankoro

Children, don't tell lies
   Akpakoro – kpankoro
Not even a small one
   Akpakoro – kpankoro

Children you'll soon grow
   Udumo – ogene
And perhaps you'll grow rich
   Udumo – ogene

Please, children, remember the poor
   Udumo – ogene
Who are not as lucky as you're
   Udumo – ogene

Akpakoro – kpankoro
Udumo – ogene
Akpakoro – kpankoro
Akpakoro – kpankoro
Udumo – ogene
Udumo – ogene

25 *A wrestling contest*

The animals once disobeyed their ancestors, and as a punishment a great famine started throughout their kingdom. There was scarcely anything to eat. Their hunger was getting to so great extent that their King organized a series of wrestling competitions.

'This is not the ideal way to solve our problem, I know, but it is about the most effective,' he told his subjects. 'Any competitor that defeats his opponent is free to kill the latter and eat him as food. If, however, the defeated wrestler offers a ransom, he may be released if the victor so wishes.'

Most animals were pleased with this arrangement. The ram and his friend, the tortoise, got ready the next day to go and try their luck. The ram defeated all his opponents and killed them. The tortoise was always defeated but not killed because of his friend's influence. It was the ram who always saved him by paying a ransom.

'Look for a competitor smaller than you are,' he warned the tortoise.

The next animal to wrestle with the tortoise was a bat. He carried the bat up and it seemed he would appear victorious, but his rival was experienced and could not be thrown down. It was the tortoise who was finally defeated. The bat picked up a sickle to kill him but the ram quickly intervened. He gave two of his games to the bat for the release of his friend. The tortoise was once again spared.

A couple of hours later he saw a very sickly goat. He asked the little goat to wrestle with him. The challenge was accepted. For the first time in his life, the tortoise emerged the victor. The mother of the sickly goat wanted to pay a ransom, but the tortoise was not ready to listen – not even to the pleadings of his friend the ram.

He quickly killed the goat and cooked the meat. He gave one ear to the ram. He waited for a modest interval, and then went to him to demand his piece of meat back. This was immediately given to him.

'I am joking, eat your meat. Let's go to the Boro Lake and drink,' the tortoise insisted.

On arrival at the lake the tortoise made certain that his friend did swallow the meat. As they were going home, the tortoise wanted back his piece of meat. The meat had already been swallowed.

'I want my meat back. Nothing but the ear of the goat I gave to you.'

The distressed ram gave him one of his games, but he refused to accept it.

'I want my meat back or all your games.'

The ram perfunctorily gave away all his games. At home he thought of ways to teach the tortoise a lesson he would never forget. Suddenly a thought came to him. He made a statue of his father with eso (a very gummy substance). He left the statue in front of this house. Late in the evening, the tortoise passed the ram's house. In spite of his sophistication and witticism, the tortoise never failed to greet his elders.

Not aware of his friend's trick, he approached the 'old man' and offered his salutation.

'Ogbuefi Ebine, igadi – O,' he said.

There was no response whatsoever.

'I say, Ogbuefi Ebine, igadi,' he repeated.

Again there was no answer. With all his might he gave the old man a slap. His hand was held by the eso. He used his left hand, and the same thing happened. Next he used his legs, which were also held fast. He shouted in agony until the ram ran out.

'You've murdered my father,' the ram shouted. 'Atami, Atami,' he called, 'Atami, bring me a sharp knife.'

'Please do not kill me,' the tortoise pleaded.

He was released when he promised to give all his property to the ram.

Now that he had lost all his property, he planned his own trick. He fashioned a statue of his grandfather with pounded cassava. He carried the statue to his friend's house and climbed a coconut tree to see what would happen.

As soon as the ram saw the statue, he knew what his friend had up his sleeve. He called on his wife:

'Atami, prepare soup immediately.'

He sent his servants to go and ask the animals to come for a meal. The statue was demolished and repounded. The guests enjoyed the food. The disappointed tortoise rushed out of his place of hiding and joined in the merry-making.

26 *Friendship without meals*

The green-turtle went to the heron and asked her to become his friend. Hitherto the heron had been very lonely; she was glad to accept the green-turtle as her friend. They ate and drank together and often played together. Since the heron was a woman, she did all the cooking, while the green-turtle provided the food. One afternoon he brought home a large quantity of fresh fish. He divided the fish in two and gave one half to the heron for their midday meal. Porridged yam was prepared. The greedy green-turtle wanted to eat the food alone and had to think of tricks.

Just as they were about to do justice to the food, he made a suggestion:

'I want each of us to call out his or her name before eating. That's what is done by all my friends and I think it is a good idea if we follow suit.'

The green-turtle, who was a good speaker, called out his name with much dexterity: GREEN-TURTLE.

The heron was a stammerer. Each attempt of hers was unsuccessful. She could only succeed in saying: HE – E – HER – RR – ON – NN.

She gave up the attempt when she found out that all the food had been eaten by her friend.

For their evening meal she used the other half of the fish to prepare rice and stew. As usual, the green-turtle thought of a trick, but this time his friend was faster. When the food was ready, she brought her suggestion.

'Did I tell you, my friend,' she started, 'that my in-laws used to wash their hands before and after a meal.'

She washed her hands and flew to the kitchen. The turtle washed his but dirtied them by the time he arrived at the kitchen.

'Go and wash your hands,' the heron instructed him.

By the time he got back his hands were dirtier than ever. He gave up the fight when she announced that there was no more food left.

In his anger he ruled that they would continue their friendship but would never eat together.

27 *The death of the fox*

Queen Camel wanted to build a palace for her husband who was on tour. She invited all her subjects to come and clear the building site for her. All the animals turned up and worked very conscientiously. It did not take long before the place was levelled up and all the tree stumps uprooted. The Queen was very much impressed, and to show her satisfaction, she gave a cow to them. The subjects were happy and said they would kill the cow on the day King Camel was due back home. The cow was, therefore, left to graze in a lush pasture.

The snail wanted to cheat all the other animals. He spent five sleepless nights thinking of how to steal the cow.

He went to the grazing field and hid himself among the tall grasses hoping the animal would engulf him with the grass when he took the next mouthful. His dream came true! The cow swallowed him with the grass. He then started feasting on his host. The cow became very lean and could no longer stand up. All the animals noticed this sudden change of condition and arrived at the conclusion that the cow should be slaughtered the next day. The next morning they gathered in the queen's palace. But one of them was missing. The snail was not there.

It was surprising that the snail should choose to be absent. For one thing he was known throughout the land for his great affinity for meat. Everyone wondered why he was not present. His wife was contacted immediately but she did not know anything about her husband's whereabouts.

The cow was killed. No-one had ever thought that the snail might be inside the cow's stomach. It was the fox who saw him when he was coming out. All of them were asked to go home and come back in the evening.

The fox was determined to divulge the secret to all the animals in the evening. In the evening the snail failed to turn up.

'I saw him playing his harp when I was coming,' said one of the animals.

Some animals were asked to go and get him. When the snail saw them coming he played a good tune. They danced and refused to go back. The fox was anxious to disclose the secret but waited for the other animals to come back with the thief. Another batch was sent, but like the first, did not return. Queen Camel was annoyed and sent another group with the lion as the leader.

From afar the lion saw them swinging and swaying. He was resolved to beat them. Hardly had he reached the scene when he started to dance to the merry tunes. He asked the snail to teach him how to play the harp. He snatched it from the owner and broke one of the strings.

'The strings are replaceable with a fox's veins,' he told the lion. The lion caught the fox and killed him and his veins were taken out. The animals – including the snail – went back to the palace, where they shared the meat among themselves.

28 *Why the wolf lives in the jungle*

Long ago the wolf was living with human beings, but unlike his neighbours, he was very lazy and did not wish to work. He believed in having a good time. When it was time to till the land he left the village lest he should be asked to work. At harvesting period he came back to beg for food. His immediate neighbour was an old woman of seventy-five, who was very industrious. She made akara (a type of cake made from beans and onions), which she carried about the village. The wolf was very fond of akara, but the old woman would not give him any.

Very early one morning he hid himself behind a mahogany

tree, awaiting the hawker's arrival. As soon as the woman was in sight, he started a song. Horrified, the woman left her wares, which the wolf devoured. The second day the same thing happened. The old woman lodged a complaint with the village chief. The chief sent a team of ten men to accompany her the next day. The men ran away when they heard the frightful but entertaining song. As usual, the wolf ate all the akara. The men reported back to the chief who selected twenty other men. These men were unsuccessful, too. He became worried and promised to reward whoever could solve the riddle. A sawyer promised to solve the mystery. He took five men with him. He took a cripple, a deaf-and-dumb man, a blind man and two medicine-men. They accompanied the old woman while she went about hawking her wares. As soon as the wolf perceived the odour of the akara, he started his usual song. The hawker and the men ran away, leaving behind the cripple, the deaf-and-dumb man and the blind man. The wolf came out to eat the akara and was caught by the deaf-and-dumb man.

He was taken to the village chief who consulted his chief advisers. The wolf was ordered to be banished from the village.

That is why the wolf no longer lives with man but stays in the jungle.

29 *Why the tortoise is often found in pits*

Nkwoagu was the biggest market in the land of the animals. Animals from the neighbouring places came to Nkwoagu to buy and sell. The tortoise knew of this and on one market day he hid himself in a dead ant-hill. When the market was in full swing he shouted:

> 'The ancestors and owners of Nkwoagu are coming.
> You've all violated the tradition.
> Nkwoagu market has been defiled;
> Calamity befalls whoever is caught.'

As soon as the animals heard this curse they fled leaving their wares behind. Their ancestors had told them that Nkwoagu was originally a place of sacrifice but had been converted into a market by the chief, much to the annoyance of the gods.

The tortoise came out and carried away the goods he fancied. At dusk the animals came back to carry away their wares. Some of them noticed that theirs had disappeared. On the next market day the tortoise sang his usual song:

> 'The ancestors and owners of Nkwoagu are coming.
> You've all violated the tradition.
> Nkwoagu market has been defiled;
> Calamity befalls whoever is caught.'

There was the usual pandemonium. The tortoise achieved his objective.

The owl volunteered to meet the evil spirit face-to-face. On the next market day he painted his face with cohise chalk and charcoal and sat at the back of the ant-hill where the tortoise was hiding. The normal bargaining and bustle of activity started.

> 'The ancestors and owners of Nkwoagu are coming.
> You've all violated the tradition.
> Nkwoagu market has been defiled;
> Calamity befalls whoever is caught.'

91

Mr Tortoise, with his usual poise, came out to gather the commodities he liked. He was caught red-handed by the owl. All the animals were summoned to decide the offender's punishment.

'The same good-for-nothing tortoise! Kill him! Kill him! No more nonsense from him,' filled the air. A death sentence was imposed on him. He was locked up in a tiny hut awaiting his execution the following day. His wife was allowed to visit him at night. He instructed her to bring 'ogiri' and rub it on him. (Ogiri is a blackish condiment made from fermented melon seeds). The wife carried out her husband's instructions.

The following morning the animals gathered to see the tortoise killed. The smell of the ogiri rubbed on his body was awful and the odour was most offensive and pungent.

'The poor beast is already dead. Throw him away.'

'Mr Millipede is right,' echoed the owl and the pigeon together.

The vulture was asked to carry the 'dead' tortoise to a near-by pit. The vulture threw the tortoise into the pit, and the latter rose up and went home. He developed a special liking for pits. Today the tortoise is often found in pits.

30 *The beetle and the wasp*

The beetle made his living by trapping animals. He set his trap near the house of the wasp and for this reason he asked the wasp to watch it for him.

'If a small animal is trapped, take it,' he advised the wasp. 'If a big one is trapped, bring it to me and I shall share it with you.'

The wasp was pleased with this arrangement but did not carry out his friend's instructions. He took the big animals and brought the small ones to the beetle. The beetle on each occasion asked him to take the little animals.

'I wonder why my trap no longer catches big animals? Is the tongue faulty, or something?'

The beetle went to examine his trap but found there was nothing wrong with it. He suspected that the wasp was deceiving him. His suspicion was confirmed when the spider told him that he had transacted business once with the wasp and found him grossly dishonest.

The beetle went to his friend the guinea-fowl and told him his trouble.

'I shall solve your problem for you,' the guinea-fowl assured him. 'Reset your trap tomorrow morning.'

The next morning he went to the trap and was caught. When the wasp saw the guinea-fowl trapped he was afraid. He refused to carry the victim home. He rushed to the beetle to ask him to come. The beetle gave him permission to carry the guinea-fowl.

'Carry me home,' the guinea-fowl advised the wasp.

He still hesitated and was struck by lightning and instantly became blind. He stooped down and carried away the guinea-fowl. He confessed that he had been cheating the beetle and promised never to be dishonest in future. He regained his sight and the guinea-fowl went to his friend to report his success.

3 1 *The origin of death*

When God created the world He left the creatures to choose whether or not there should be death. There were two groups of living creatures, human beings and the lower animals. God asked the two groups to decide amongst themselves whether death should be in existence. All the living creatures held a meeting and the majority of them decided that there should be no death. A few others, led by the crocodile, maintained that there should be death. Since they were the minority group, the crocodile and his supporters kept quiet.

The dog was sent to inform God that there should be no death. On the way he saw bones and stopped to eat them. He was so carried away by the sweetness of the bones that he forgot his mission to God. The crocodile saw him eating and immediately sent the frog to tell God that there should be death. This the frog did.

When the dog finished with the bones, he ran to deliver the message. God told him that he was too late and that He had already created death.

That is how death came about.

3 2 *The origin of the tortoise's shell*

The tortoise sent his son to get some live coal from the woodpecker's house. When he arrived there he found the owner of the house roasting palm fruits. The woodpecker gave

94

three to the tortoise's son. The latter took the fruits home and gave one to his father. The tortoise was pleased with the delicious taste of this succulent fruit. He sent his son to the woodpecker's house again. As soon as the son left he made up his mind to follow him. Mr Woodpecker roasted more fruits for his two uninvited guests.

'From where did you get these fruits?' the anxious tortoise queried.

'Don't worry. I shall bring you some if you'll bring me a bag tomorrow.'

The tortoise went away satisfied. The next day he brought a big old bag and entered into it. He asked his son to take the bag to the woodpecker. Who took it and flew to the palm tree from where he got the first fruits. He wondered why the tortoise chose to bring a heavy bag. He placed the fruits into the bag as soon as he got them. Meanwhile, the tortoise was greedily eating the fruits and throwing away the kernels through a little opening he had made.

The woodpecker became irritated and very impatient. It was taking him a long time to fill up the bag. He flung it open and saw the tortoise eating the fruits. He took hold of him and threw him into a river that was nearby. The tortoise appealed to a shoal of fish to come to his aid.

'If you bring me to the bank,' he said, 'I shall make you all longer and more beautiful than you are.'

The fish quickly hurled him to the bank. He collected faggots and made a fire. He jumped over the fire and asked the fish to follow suit. The first fish jumped, fell into the fire and was stretched as it lay lifeless.

'See how tall and beautiful this fish is,' he remarked.

The second fish jumped and died. One by one all of them jumped over the fire and were killed. The tortoise collected them and parcelled them in leaves and went away. On the way he was stopped by a tiger who wanted to know what he was carrying.

'I'm carrying the body of my father.'

The tiger expressed his sympathy and went away. A leopard met him and was told the same story. The tortoise increased his speed. Soon a lion stopped him. He told the inquisitive lion that he was carrying the body of his dead father.

'In our village one man does not bury the dead alone. I shall help you.'

The tortoise did not need any help but he dared not say so, lest the lion should molest him.

'Let me answer my ancestors,' he told the lion.

The lion waited for him while he entered the forest to ease himself. When he had finished he placed red pepper on his defecation and went away.

'Mr Tortoise! Mr Tortoise!' the impatient lion called. He went to look for him. 'Mr Tortoise! Mr Tortoise!

The human refuse answered:

'I'm coming.'

The lion soon discovered the trick and quickly traced the whereabouts of his companion by following his footprints. The footprints brought him to the house of the tortoise, where the latter was sitting cosily, eating his fish. The lion was infuriated.

'So this is where you've been burying your father?' he questioned him.

He covered the tortoise with a mortar and ate all the fish. He forgot to let him out when he was about to leave. The tortoise had to move about with the mortar on top of him. He became a shelled creature.

33 *The emu disgraced*

The emu was eating in his house when he accidentally swallowed a small bone. He tried to remove it but could not. He went to all his friends but none could give him the help he so desperately needed. Some, in their attempts to bring out the bone, pushed it further in. He promised to give his daughter in marriage to any bird that could rid him of the bone. Many birds tried to remove the bone so as to marry his daughter. A friend came to visit him one evening. He was surprised to find the emu in distress and he suggested that the kiwi should be notified.

'When my mother swallowed a pointed bone two years ago, everyone thought she would die. It was the kiwi that saved her life.'

The kiwi was informed of the accident. He placed his long beak into the emu's mouth and brought out the bone. The emu said he was grateful, but refused to give his daughter in marriage to the kiwi.

'You knew you could save me but you didn't care to come. You wanted me to suffer first.'

The emu could not be moved. All the other birds appealed to him, but he would not change his mind.

Eight months passed and the kiwi started paying frequent visits to the emu's family. It was not long before he became friendly with the emu again. However, he still nursed an ill-feeling for him. He was simply looking for a way to revenge himself on him. The opportunity he was looking for came. The falcon married a new wife and invited all the birds to come and rejoice with him. Both the emu and the kiwi were invited, and coincidentally, both of them were given the same dish of food.

97

There was plenty to eat and drink and the emu was among the first to become intoxicated. The kiwi took a hook-shaped bone and placed it in their dish. He asked his drunken companion to eat. The latter swallowed the food and the bone. The drunkenness disappeared as he ran hither and thither asking for help. The other birds accused him of greed. The only bird that could help him was the kiwi, but he refused to help.

The emu's poor voice was brought about by this bone which was never removed.

34 *The tortoise proves his intelligence*

Many animals believed that the tortoise was the wisest animal that ever lived. One day the King wanted to see if the tortoise merited this title. He sent for the tortoise and gave him a piece of yam saying:

'I shall officially declare you the wisest animal alive if you can buy a house with this piece of yam. In addition, I shall make you my principal adviser.'

The tortoise scratched his head and went away with the piece of yam. He told his wife he knew a place where yams were very costly. At dusk he set out for the unknown place. When he could no longer continue because of darkness, he entered a house that was nearby, and told the owner of the house – a farmer – that he too was a farmer and an accomplished traveller. He was warmly received and given food to eat. He showed his host the piece of yam which he claimed could feed a whole village when boiled.

'I told you I'm a traveller. God gave me this piece of yam when I went to visit Him in heaven.'

The farmer marvelled at the strange powers of the little

yam. The tortoise left the yam on the floor when he went to bed. A goat ate it during the night. In the morning the tortoise told his host that he (the tortoise) would die if he did not recover that piece of yam.

'Take the goat with you,' the farmer advised him, 'when you get home you can kill it and recover your yam.'

The tortoise was happy. He left to continue his journey. At nightfall he entered the first house he saw. The owner of the house was a gamekeeper. He was known throughout the land for his kindness to people, especially strangers. He did all he could to make his guest feel at home. He had many houses, some of which sheltered his animals. During the night one of his lions killed the goat.

'I am dead,' the tortoise sobbed.

The gamekeeper promised to buy him a new goat but he objected.

'This particular goat was bought for an exchange of a house with a friend living many miles from here,' he told his host.

The gamekeeper gave him one of his many houses, and the tortoise went to report his success to the King. The King made investigations and found that the story was true. He proclaimed the tortoise the wisest animal and made him his principal adviser.

35 *The result of envy*

A boy once went to the farm with his parents. Their farm was two miles away and since they left very early in the morning, they carried food with them. They worked very hard and when the sun appeared they sat down to take their breakfast. Their son, Oko, had a whistle with him. While his parents relaxed, he played beautiful songs on his whistle.

'Drop that whistle, Oko,' his mother urged him.

When the relaxation was over they started working again. Now and then Oko stood up to play a tune or two.

'The sun is setting, ma and pa,' Oko reminded his parents.

They collected their farm implements and mama Oko gathered pieces of wood for cooking. On their way home, Oko shouted that he had forgotten his whistle. He wanted to go back to the farm but his father refused to let him, telling him he would make him a new one at home.

'If you'll make a new one for me, I shall then have two,' Oko replied.

'If you want two whistles, I shall make two for you at home.'

Still Oko was not satisfied and continued:

'If you make two whistles for me, I shall then have three. I can't leave my whistle behind. That's very unfair.'

Oko was given the permission he wanted. When he arrived at the farm he found seven spirits dancing and asked them melodiously:

> 'Spirits, did you see my whistle?
> Zamiriza
> The whistle I forgot in our farm?
> Zamiriza
> I've come to take it home,
> Zamiriza.'

The spirits replied, still dancing:

> 'Little boy, your whistle has gone,
> Sawam

> Our King has taken it
> Sawam
> We shall take you to his palace,
> Sawam.'

Oko was taken to their King. He was asked to sit down on a gold-lined mat, but he refused.

'I'm a poor boy from a poor family. I'm accustomed to using mats made with straw or hay.'

The little boy's simplicity charmed the King. He was asked to sleep on a bed, but he chose a mat instead. In the morning, he was shown three whistles – whistles made of gold, plastic and wood. He chose the wooden one as his. The King said he would reward him generously. He brought out an old pot and gave it to him.

'Break this pot in front of your father's house,' the King advised him.

Oko thanked him and went home. He broke the pot as directed and miraculously, their mud house was transformed into a modern house. The floor was covered with money.

His parents became rich and called their friends to celebrate their good luck with them. The guests were told how the wealth came about. One woman called Akunkwo, was not pleased. The next day she took her son, Nkachi, and her husband to the farm. She left Nkachi's whistle in the farm, and on the way home she asked him to go back to the farm for it. Nkachi saw seven spirits dancing when he arrived, but unlike Oko, he did not sing. He simply asked them to take him to their King. The spirits obeyed and took him to their King. He chose a brand-new mat instead of the old one that was offered to him. He slept on the King's bed without being told to do so, and in the morning he demanded a pot.

He was presented with two and he chose the new one.

'When you reach home,' the King began, 'ask your . . .'

'I know the directions,' Nkachi interrupted him.

He thanked the King and went home. His mother ran to meet him when she saw him carrying a pot. She took the pot from him and smashed it on the ground. Almost immediately their mud house fell and she was killed. Nkachi escaped with a few bruises.

36 *The millipede's blindness*

The cat was tired of living alone and for this reason he wanted to get married. He had his eye on the most beautiful girl in the community. When he had saved enough money for the dowry, he asked some of his friends to escort him to Chief Rabbit's house.

'I have come to marry your daughter,' he addressed the Chief.

Chief Rabbit brushed aside his long whiskers and stared at the cat out of the corners of his eyes.

'Well, well, well,' he began, 'it all depends on my daughter. If she accepts you I shan't have any objections.'

Miss Rabbit was called and asked if she would like to marry the cat. She nodded and said she would, but remarked that she would marry him on the condition that he changed the colour of his eyes.

'I am terrified of those ferret-red eyes of his,' she concluded.

'Gentlemen,' Chief Rabbit commenced, 'you've all heard what my daughter said.'

The cat and his companions announced that they would come back on the next market day. That night he could not sleep. The thought of losing the most beautiful bride in the village filled him with tears. He went to the turkey the next day. He wanted the turkey to lend him a pair of eyes, but the turkey bluntly refused. He went to the millipede and told him his trouble.

'I once lent my eyes to someone but he refused to return them to me. I had to plead before I got my own eyes back.'

'That's most unfortunate. You remember the saying "One dirty finger soon dirties the rest"?'

The millipede was not moved by the cat's reply.

'I'm sorry, I cannot help you, Mr Cat.'

After shedding 'crocodile' tears, the cat went away. Very early the next morning he came again. The millipede was still sleeping. He waited till his creditor-to-be woke up. The cat knelt down in front of the millipede and asked him to grant his request. The millipede's heart was softened. He asked his debtor to come in the evening and take the eyes. Sunset saw the cat in the millipede's house.

'Return them to me first thing tomorrow morning,' said the millipede.

The cat swore that he would return them. He went to Chief Rabbit's house. Miss Rabbit was happy to see that her suitor's eyes had become normal.

'I am going home with you this night,' she shouted to the cat.

The dowry was paid and he took Miss Rabbit with him. His joy knew no bounds. He was the husband of the most beautiful girl in the hamlet.

'If I return these eyes to the millipede,' he reasoned within himself, 'I may lose my wife.'

The next day he packed bag and baggage and went to

103

another hamlet with his wife. The millipede groped his way to the cat's house but found that it was deserted. He made enquiries about his debtor's whereabouts, but could get no satisfactory answer. He went home blaming himself for his folly. The millipede has been a blind creature since then.

37 *The volunteer*

The eagle summoned all his subjects. He told them that for a long time there had been no rain and human beings were encountering untold hardship.

'The only way of helping them,' the eagle continued, 'is by sending a gift to our ancestors in the sky. I want one of you to volunteer to take the offering to the sky.'

There was an uneasy silence as everyone sat tongue-tied.

'Why bother yourself with what does not concern you, King Eagle?' the vulture asked.

There was dead silence.

'I hope your majesty is not sleeping?' the vulture put in, rather satirically.

'Your question was heard, Mr Vulture,' the eagle replied. 'You see, our neighbours (men) sent delegates to me asking for my help. Any volunteers, gentlemen and ladies?'

There was no response. The King pointed at the snake and asked him to volunteer.

'Your majesty has forgotten that I am no good at flying,' the snake replied.

'You try,' the eagle told the weaver-bird.

The weaver-bird excused herself by saying that her labour would start in a few minutes time.

'What do you say, Mr Crane?' King Eagle continued.

'I have just returned from my world tour. Will you not give me time to rest?'

'Leave Mr Crane! Leave Mr Crane!' the other animals pleaded.

'You look prepared to go, Mr Winter-bird?'

The winter-bird shook his head and suggested that the vulture should go: 'Good old Mr Vulture. He is always a helpful and active member of our society,' the crow added.

'Thank you, Mr Vulture,' the others concluded.

The King praised the vulture and said he was very popular; otherwise, all the birds could not have reposed such confidence in him.

The vulture set off the next day. On his way back, rain fell and disfigured him. The rainfall was so heavy that he lost all the feathers on his neck and head. When he came back all his comrades laughed at him and called him a scavenger.

This incident accounts for the vulture's partial baldness.

38 Tit for tat

The vulture had a big farm which yielded a good harvest annually. He was a farmer by profession and spent the greater part of his time guarding the farm. Many animals envied him. The chimpanzee fought tooth and nail to claim ownership of this farm.

He passed one afternoon and observed that the vulture was not there. He entered stealthily and sat down. The vulture was surprised to find the chimpanzee sitting in his farm.

'What are you doing here, Mr Chimpanzee?' he asked in anger.

'Will you get out of here?' the chimpanzee replied, 'this farm belongs to me.'

The vulture reported the incident to the village Council. Proof of ownership was demanded, but the owner could not produce any.

'Show us the pathway you normally take on entering the farm,' the Councillors requested.

The vulture could not do this, since he flew in and out of the farm. The chimpanzee was declared the rightful owner as soon as he showed the pathways he took. The vulture went away dissatisfied.

The chimpanzee was by profession a retailer. Two years after the dispute with the vulture, he went to a distant land and bought goods to be retailed. The vulture heard of it and waited for him. When the chimpanzee returned he went up to him and helped him with his heavy goods. The chimpanzee had forgotten everything about their quarrel and was pleased with the vulture. To his surprise, however, he noticed that the vulture was carrying the commodities to his own house. He reported the 'theft' to the Council, and as usual, owner-ship of the goods would have to be shown.

The chimpanzee opened his mouth and then closed it. The vulture showed his bald head which he claimed was caused by the weight of the goods. He argued further that only the rightful owner of the goods could afford to carry the heavy load. He was given ownership of the goods. He sold them and bought a dozen new farms with the money.

39 *The chameleon's power of changing colours*

The chameleon and the lizards were bitter enemies. The lizards laughed at him each time they saw him and called him all sorts of names. The chameleon was by nature a very shy creature, and resented this attitude of his neighbours. He packed up and went away to get a new house, but when he was unable to find one, he went back to the old one which he shared with the lizards. There was no-one to keep him company and life was becoming a burden too heavy for him to bear.

He went to the egret and told him his trouble. The egret promised to help him.

'I shall give you the power to go about unnoticed,' the egret consoled him.

He took the chameleon to a deserted lake. He picked some leaves and crushed them and gave them to him to chew. As soon as he chewed these leaves, he possessed the power to change to any colour he wanted. Another effect of the leaves was that the chameleon could now produce poison with which to kill his enemies.

When he came back he killed a great many lizards with this poison. The lizards became afraid of the chameleon's new powers and appealed to their King to intervene. King Lizard

107

called the chameleon to his palace, but the latter refused to go. The lizards left where they were living and went to live on the walls and ceilings of houses.

This story explains firstly, how the chameleon came to possess the power of changing his colour and secondly, why lizards live on walls and ceilings.

40 *A fight in the sky*

Famine was the commonest trouble the animals had. There was no year that ended without two or three periods of famine. Usually there was famine after each annual *emumeji*. This festival was held for the sole purpose of offering sacrifices to their ancestors. But this year's *emumeji* was different. There was no food or fruit to offer to their ancestors. Contrary to everyone's expectations, famine had preceded the *emumeji*. All the animals were starving except the squirrel. His mother was in the sky, and at each meal time he went to the sky to eat with her. The tortoise was quick to notice this. He therefore made friends with the squirrel, who promised to share his meals with him.

In the morning they set out together. When they arrived at a certain spot the squirrel sang a song.

> 'Mother, Mother!
> Titiro
> I am here
> Titiro

> Open for me
> Titiro'.

Immediately a long rope came down and the two friends went up to the sky. After they had had their meal they came down. In the afternoon the tortoise collected as many animals as he could find and they went to have their meal in the sky. The tortoise knew the song:

> 'Mother, Mother!
> Titiro
> I am here
> Titiro
> Open for me
> Titiro'.

The rope came down and the animals started climbing. The tortoise took the lead, followed by the lion. They were half-way when the squirrel was informed of the looming danger to his ageing mother. He ran to the scene and sang:

> 'Mother, Mother!
> Ajambene
> Mother, Mother,
> Ajambene
> Cut the rope,
> Ajambene
> Enemies are coming
> Ajambene.'

The rope was cut and the animals came crashing to the ground. Ten of them were killed. These were carried away by the others and dried for future use. The hippopotamus, because of his size, was asked to keep watch over the meat. At night the tortoise stole in and ate a part of the meat. The

Animals climb up to the sky
with the aid of a long rope

110

hippopotamus was killed when he could not give a satisfactory explanation of the theft. It was the antelope's turn to watch. He too, was asleep when the tortoise came in. He was killed the next morning. Next to watch was the owl. He knew the thief would come out at night and armed himself. At midnight a terrible gust of wind blew. The owl knew that the rogue was coming. The leaves of trees rustled and the stillness of the night was disturbed. He picked up his bow and arrow and hid behind a tree. A quaint figure was approaching. The face was hooded and everything about him was black.

'This is the thief coming,' the owl told himself.

The quaint figure entered the apartment where the meat was kept. The owl released his arrow and it hit the rogue on the head. Before the night-watchman could aim again, the rogue had vanished. Early in the morning the owl summoned all the animals and narrated the story of the previous night's incidents. All the animals were present and an identification parade was arranged. Some of the animals had hats on. The tortoise refused to remove his but the lion was instructed to remove it by force. It was evident from the wound on his head that he was the rogue. It was decided that he should be thrown away into a deep pit to die.

'Please don't throw me on soft ground,' he begged those going to throw him away, 'otherwise I shall die. Leave me on hard ground, so that I can live.'

'We want you to die,' the animals replied.

They threw him into a muddy pit where they thought he would die, but as soon as they went away, he came out and walked away, singing merrily.

41 *The ram is engaged in a combat*

The ram's mother was very poor. She could hardly get enough food for herself and her son. She was fond of her son and did not want him to die of hunger, and because of this, she had to apprentice him to the flamingo. Mr Flamingo had earlier told her that he was looking for a cook.

'Can you cook well?' the flamingo queried the new-comer.

'People say I am an excellent cook!'

The first meal the ram prepared was condemned by his master.

'I'm a cattle rearer and there is nothing I need more than a good meal to keep me going. My work is tedious and my hours are long, and that is why I have employed you. If you can't cook I shall send you back to your mother.'

Very early in the morning the next day, the flamingo went to tap wine. The ram slashed open the stomach of one of the cattle and brought out its intestines. He then dug four holes and pushed the limbs of the dead cow into these holes so that it could still stand erect. He prepared the breakfast with the meat but ate the meat alone so that his master would not find out. When the flamingo came back he praised the ram for the nice breakfast.

'You're a wonderful cook, my son,' he complimented him.

For each meal the ram killed a cow until all the animals were dead. A few days later his master came home very tired. He went to milk the cows for fresh milk to drink. Each cow he touched fell down. He shouted and his neighbour, the wine-tapper, came to find out what was wrong. The flamingo pointed at his cattle, surprised. He was told that the ram was responsible for the death of the cattle. The ram was called and questioned.

112

'Do you think I've been preparing those nice meals with my fingers?' he asked his master arrogantly.

The flamingo picked up a knife and drove him away.

It was not difficult for the ram to get apprenticed to another person, this time to a medicine-man. Mr Okwari was a re-nowned native doctor and he promised to teach his trade to the ram. He had a big old leather bag which contained all his tools of trade, and the ram was made the custodian of this bag.

One day the Okwari fell ill. Leaves and herbs were collected and a great fire made for him. He sat near the fire snoring. It went out as soon as all the firewood was used up. To keep it going, the ram threw his master's bag and its contents into the fire. When Okwari recovered from his illness, he was told that his bag had been burnt. He was mad with anger and threatened the ram with death. The ram packed his belongings and ran home to his mother.

The lion came to take him as a servant. He had once been victimized by the ram's father, and now that the father was dead, he felt it was a good opportunity to revenge himself on the ram.

'I have heard all the things you did to your former masters. I want to assure you right away, that you cannot behave in that fashion in my house.'

The ram did not respond. He knew he was too tough for the lion.

The lion had one son, Nwagu. The three of them slept to-gether. The lion slept in the centre, with his son, Nwagu, on his right and the ram on his left. On the third night the lion planned to kill the ram and painted the ram's face black with charcoal and painted Nwagu's face white with cohise chalk.

The ram knew of this plan and did not go to sleep. When he saw that the lion was fast asleep, he washed his face and re-painted it white. He cleaned Nwagu's face and painted it

113

black with charcoal. He then changed positions with Nwagu. A little before dawn, the lion woke up and killed his son, thinking the ram was still at his left hand. He roasted the meat and gave some to the ram.

'Say "we have killed the ram, the son of Chief Ebineako",' he instructed the ram, whom he thought was his son.

In the morning the lion went to tap wine. The ram washed his face and came out and stood near the palm tree.

'Stupid lion, we have eaten the meat of your son.'

The lion looked down and was surprised to see the ram alive. He realized immediately that he had killed his own son. He threw his knife at the ram, who artfully dodged away. In his great fury he threw himself at him but fell on the hard ground and broke his neck. He died the next day. The ram had already gone back to his mother.

42 *The magic oil*

The mosquito was once living with the spirits. He was employed as a domestic. Often he was sent to far lands and to facilitate the execution of his job, he was given a horse. The queen of the Spirits was fond of him and treated him with kindness. She had been pregnant for a long time and when it was evident that her labour was about to start, the mosquito was sent to the land of the animals to call the heifer.

On arrival he told the heifer that the queen of the Spirits

wanted her to come without delay. The heifer hurriedly dressed herself and joined the mosquito on the horse. On the way the mosquito stopped and talked to the heifer.

'If you are given any food or gift, do not accept or else you'll find yourself in trouble,' he warned her.

The heifer was still pondering over these words when the mosquito stopped and tethered the horse near a little cave.

'This way, Miss Heifer,' he instructed his companion.

The heifer marvelled at the cleanliness of the cave. It was unlike any cave she had seen before. It was brightly lit and the entrance was decorated with flowers. She was greeted by five spirits. Two of these spirits had four heads and three legs each, but the other three had ten legs and no heads. Heifer's head was swollen with fear.

She was rushed to the queen whose labour had just started. The heifer helped her with the delivery. She washed and powdered the baby. The queen brought an evil-smelling pomade, which she requested the 'mid-wife' to rub on the baby's face. This pomade enabled anyone on whose face it was rubbed, to see beyond the land of the spirits. Such a person would, as it were, live in a double world. He could see what was going on all over the earth. The heifer scratched her eyebrow and immediately she discovered she was able to see more than she did before. She refused all the gifts that were offered to her.

On her way home she told the mosquito what had happened.

'Five years ago I ate food with one of the spirits, and ever since than I have not been able to go home,' explained the mosquito.

The heifer removed the little pomade that stuck on her eyebrow and rubbed it on the mosquito's face. The mosquito was then able to see what the spirits saw. His new intelligence was recognized by all the spirits, and in no time at all he was installed as the King of the Spirits. But, one condition necessary

for the kingship, was that the King should not feed on anything else but human blood. The mosquito accepted this
condition and received the kingship.

Since that time the mosquito has lived exclusively on human
blood.

43 *The maltreated child*

The land of Lolo was ruled by a king called King Fortune.
He had a pretty wife and a daughter named Awuka. Awuka was
a charming princess and was the royal couple's main joy. Un-
expectedly the queen took ill and died. King Fortune became
a miserable sovereign. He could not cope with his royal duties
without the comforting care of a wife. Awuka too, was ill with
grief. The King was advised by his courtiers to marry a new
wife who would take care of Awuka.

The princess the King married was very fond of girls and
loved Awuka tenderly. When she became pregnant she prayed
that her baby should be a female. Her prayer was answered:
Enutrof gave birth to a baby girl.

Her child grew up a very beautiful girl. She was not, however,
as beautiful as her mother wanted her to be. Moreover, she
was nothing when compared with the ever-elegant Awuka.
Enutrof became unfriendly and extremely aggressive to her
step-daughter. She maltreated her. A war broke out between
Lolo and Dajaruna and King Fortune was killed. Enutrof's
hatred for her step-daughter reached its zenith during the
following two months. She occasionally starved the orphan
and used the cane with the same relish as schoolmasters always

116

did. Each time the queen went to the market she bought apples for her daughter, but none for Awuka. She chose to buy apples because she knew her step-daughter was very fond of them.

One morning Awuka picked up a rotten apple thrown away by her half-sister, and buried it in the ground, singing in a meloncholy tone:

> 'My apple tree grow,
>> Nda – a
> Grow, grow, grow
>> Nda – a
> Grow for the fatherless,
>> Nda – a
> Grow for the motherless
>> Nda – a.'

Immediately the apple tree grew and became a mighty tree. She continued her song:

> 'My apple tree produce fruits,
>> Nda – a
> Produce fruits for me, an orphan
>> Nda – a.'

All of a sudden, the tree became laden with apples.

> 'My apple fruits ripen
>> Nda – a
> Ripen for me, an orphan
>> Nda – a.'

The apples became very red but Awuka could not climb to get them. She sang again:

> 'My apple fruits fall,
>> Nda – a

> Fall for me, an orphan,
> > Nda – a
> Da – a, da – a, da – a
> > Nda – a
> Da – a, da – a, da – a
> > Nda – a.'

The apples fell from the tree. Queen Enutrof heard the noise and came out. She was surprised to see what had happened. She felt her step-daughter was more than a mortal being. She fell down and begged Awuka to forgive her. From that day she ceased her maltreatment.

44 *The elephant and the tortoise*

There was manual work to be done for the King of the animals. The King promised to pay thirty cowrie shells to any animal that volunteered to do the work. In addition, he promised to give food to the worker. The tortoise and his friend the elephant went to the King to say they were ready to do the work. They were given farm implements and taken to the farm. After every thirty minutes the tortoise went away. He either said he was going to ease himself or he was going to have a little rest. The elephant was dissatisfied with his companion's attitude. He decided to play his own tricks. He dropped his knife and went away.

'I am going to drink water,' he informed his companion.

As soon as he had left, the King and his wife arrived. The tortoise saw them and started working hard.

'Well done, Mr Tortoise! Where is your companion, Mr Elephant?'

'He said the work was very difficult and went away,' the tortoise answered.

The queen was annoyed with the elephant's attitude. She gave the tortoise the food she had brought for the two workers. The tortoise ate one half of it and left the other half, which he brought out when his friend came back. The elephant rejected the food on the grounds that it was very small. The tortoise insisted that they should take the food like that. In the evening they went to the King to get the reward promised. They were given forty cowrie shells, each of them receiving twenty.

'I want to buy a dress for my wife. Can you escort me, please?' the tortoise requested his friend.

The two companions went to a night market. The dress he wanted to buy was sold at forty cowrie shells. He borrowed twenty cowries from the elephant.

'Come tomorrow and I shall pay you,' the tortoise instructed him.

The elephant failed to go the next morning. When he went in the evening he was told there was no money.

'You failed to come at the time I asked you to,' the tortoise remarked.

He did not want to pay the elephant. An idea came to him. He advised Alia – his wife – to cover him with clayey soil and use him as a grinding stone when the elephant came the next morning.

The next morning, the elephant came as he had been instructed. Alia told him the tortoise was seriously ill and had gone to see a medicine-man. She started grinding some leaves.

'Have you any manners?' the elephant asked. 'I'm talking to you and you are not paying attention.'

119

In his rage he snatched the 'grinding-stone' from Alia and threw it away. The tortoise washed himself clean and came back. He asked what the matter was, and Alia told him.

'Go and get my grinding stone, and come back for your money.'

The elephant went to look for the grinding-stone, but couldn't find it. He forfeited his money since he could not produce the grinding-stone he had thrown away.

45 *The rat and the tortoise*

A hunting expedition was arranged by the animals. Only the tortoise refused to take part. He argued that he was ill. His decision was not taken lightly by other animals. Realizing that he was being misunderstood, he went to his most influential friend, the rat.

'I want you to convince your colleagues that I am seriously ill,' he suggested to the rat.

The animals were told by the rat that the tortoise was ill. When they left for the jungle, the tortoise went and hid himself behind an ant-hill. As soon as he saw the animals returning, he spoke to them:

'Chief Ezeanu is speaking,
You have all offended me.
Leave some of your games for me.'

The squirrel was the first animal to drop his games. He took to his heels and the tortoise came out and carried away the meat. Next came the ostrich. When he heard the voice, he dropped all he had and ran away. Ezeanu was their first ancestor, and even though he was dead, he was still revered by all. The rat was the last animal to return. He heard the voice but refused to obey. Instead, he hid himself behind a tree. As before, the tortoise came out to carry his games. The rat caught him red-handed. The offender divided the games into three, and gave two portions to the rat with the plea that he should not tell anyone what he had seen. The rat promised to keep the incident secret.

The tortoise was still worried. The only security he could have would be to kill the rat, he told himself. He gave the games to his wife to prepare bread-fruit. Bread-fruit was never prepared with meat but he was prepared to experiment on the novelty. The food was extremely sweet and delicious. He invited all the animals – but individually.

The squirrel was the first to arrive. In fact, this animal was respected throughout the land for his punctuality and sense of time. He was entertained and the host promised to give him one lump of the fruit.

'One queer thing about my bread-fruit tree is that the fruit never touches the ground. Two people are needed to get the fruits. One climbs the tree, gets the fruit and throws it to the other person on the ground.'

The squirrel said he was ready to help. The two of them went to the back of the house. The tortoise climbed the tree, plucked one fruit and threw it down to his companion.

'Catch it!' he shouted. 'Don't let it touch the ground.'

The fruit fell on the squirrel and he was killed. The tortoise came down and carried the carcass away. One after another the other animals came, and met the same fate. The last animal to come was the rat. What a coincidence! The tortoise took his guest to the bread-fruit tree. He plucked the fruit and aimed at the rat. The rat escaped death but lay flat on the ground pretending he was dead. The tortoise carried him away. He placed the 'dead' rat in a pot and covered it. A few minutes later he came to put the pot on the fire. As soon as he opened the pot the rat held him by the neck and strangled him to death.

The rat came out of the pot and carried away all the dead animals. To crown it all, he took the tortoise's wife home and Alia became his wife.

46 *Vengeance*

Old tiger was terribly thirsty. He badly wanted a drink but could not get any nearby. He had to satisfy his thirst. He climbed hills and slopes and did other manoevures searching for a pool of water. Water was hard to come by because of the long period of drought.

Presently he came to a wet area.

'There must be water somewhere around this spot,' he comforted himself, as he continued his search.

It was not long before he came to a little stream. He thanked his ancestors and started drinking copiously. He was at the elevated part of the stream. The water was flowing from his side down to the other end. When he had quenched his thirst he took time to look around him. The water was clean and there were only a few water weeds bordering the edges of the stream. Suddenly he saw the zebra drinking at the lower end of the stream. He went to her.

'Say, zebra, why do you drop particles of dirt into the water? Don't you see how you are contaminating the water for me?'

'I beg your pardon, sir,' the frightened zebra responded, 'the water flows from your own side down to mine.'

'Oh yes! I remember,' the tiger continued, 'your father punished me last week.'

The zebra looked astonished.

'My father? My father died when I was very small.'

'I am sorry; it was not your father. It was your mother. I am certain of it.'

The zebra looked more astonished than before.

'You are mistaken, sir,' she continued in self-defence. 'My mother died ten years ago.'

'I don't care who it was,' the tiger asserted: with a spring he pounced on the zebra and tore her into pieces.

47 *How the pigeon started flying*

The duck and the flamingo were reputable farmers. They produced mainly cassava, which they sold in the market. At times they went to distant places to sell their surplus goods. This year they produced maize as well as cassava, and took the maize to the market but no-one wanted to buy. They had to carry it to a market ten miles away where an acute shortage of maize was reported.

Very early in the morning they set out on their journey. They had covered half the distance before nightfall, but they could not continue because of the total darkness. They were strangers to the village where they found themselves.

Were they to sleep near the shrine of the village? Thieves might carry away their maize and money. They could neither go back to their own village nor continue their journey because of the complete darkness. They decided to enter a nearby house and spend the night with its owner. They knocked on the door and the owner of the house came out. He welcomed the strangers and gave them a room. After giving them food, he bade them goodnight.

'Where shall we leave our money?' the duck questioned his companion.

'In our baskets of maize.'

The host and hostess overheard this conversation, and at midnight they crept into the room and stole their guests' money.

'Our money has disappeared!' the duck and flamingo reported to their host and hostess early the next morning.

The host and hostess pretended to be worried by the theft, and went to their Chief to report the incident.

'This is very bad,' the Chief said, 'for a traveller to come to my land and be robbed of his possessions.'

He conducted a number of investigations, but the robber could not be traced. The Chief offered a prize to any of his subjects who could find the robber. Still there was no success. The Chief then went to his neighbours, the animals who could not fly. He had often been told that most of these animals were very intelligent. He offered a reward to any of them that could help him.

'I shall give the person the power to fly like us,' he assured the audience.

The pigeon volunteered to track down the criminal. He

went to the two farmers and gave them a bell. He took them to the village market square.

'I want you to go back to your host with this bell on your head. If you did not lose any money, the bell will ring. But if you did, the bell will not ring.'

The two farmers carried out the pigeon's instructions. Meanwhile, the pigeon had hidden himself, watching the progress of his plan. The bell did not ring and he concluded that the duck and the flamingo had really lost their money. The host and hostess were taken to the market square and given a similar instruction.

'I want you to go home with this bell. The bell will ring if you are responsible for the theft; if you are not, it will not ring.'

On the way the husband and wife started disputing between themselves.

'But you're responsible for the theft,' the wife pointed out to him.

To prevent it ringing, the man took the bell from his wife's head. Instantly it rang and the pigeon came out from his place of hiding and arraigned them.

He reported his success to the Chief who rewarded him by giving him the power to grow wings and fly.

48 *The goat's stupidity*

The goat was awaiting the return of his son, whom he had sent to buy food. For a long time the goat and members of his family had not taken any food. They had no food and no money with which to buy it. As he sat struggling with hunger, a little mouse passed his house. This mouse carried food. The goat ran out and requested the mouse to give him a little food. The mouse refused his request. He could only give the food to the goat if the latter would agree to wrestle with him. The goat was feeling hungry but somehow it occurred to him that he would easily defeat the little mouse.

The mouse left the food on the ground and the competition started. With one finger the mouse threw his opponent on the hard ground. The goat was dumbfounded. He could not believe it. As soon as the goat landed on the ground the victor carried his food and went down a deep hole that was nearby.

'Give me a second chance,' the goat pleaded.

The mouse came out again and wrestled with him. As before, the goat found himself on the ground. The mouse had run away with the food.

The goat called his wife and gave her a basket.

'As soon as we start the competition, cover this big hole with the basket I have given you.'

The mouse was beckoned to and he came out again. It did not take him any time to throw the goat. The goat stood bleating. His wife laughed when she saw her husband lifted up in the air like a small child. In her laughter she forgot to carry out her husband's instructions.

'You foolish woman, what have you been doing to forget what I told you to do?' he admonished his wife, when he noticed the mouse had escaped.

He called the duck to help. The duck too, in his laughter, forgot to discharge his duty. The goat looked for his friend the hare. The hare promised to co-operate with him on the condition that they would share the food together. This condition was acceptable to the goat.

As soon as the contest started the hare covered the hole with a basket. The mouse came to enter his hole but found that it had been blocked. He left his food and ran away. The goat carried the food to his house and started eating. He did not allow the hare to partake of the meal. The hare scratched his head and went away.

'All the bad things you've done will remain with you,' he cursed him.

This curse is responsible for the goat's stupidity.

49 *The visitors that never came*

Old Nambe told his wife Okembe that he was expecting some very important visitors. He gave her money to buy meat and fish and prepare a good soup for the visitors. The wife went to the market and came back with the ingredients necessary for the meal. She entered the kitchen and prepared the soup. She also pounded yam for the visitors. When everything was ready she went to the farm with her husband. They started uprooting cassava.

'Hush, I think I hear a noise,' Nambe told his wife. 'I'd better find out as it is possible that our visitors have arrived.'

He dropped his knife and ran home. He did not see anyone, but instead of going back to the farm, he brought out the food and ate. He poured water and soup all over the floor, then went to the farm. Their visitors had come and gone, he told his wife.

'Why did you not call me to welcome them?' Okembe wanted to know.

'I'm sorry, my dear wife, they were in a hurry.'

When they came home from the farm, Nambe complained that their visitors were careless people. He showed Okembe the pools of water on the floor. The following week he announced that the same visitors were coming. Everything was ready before they left for the farm. He told his wife that he had a feeling that the visitors had come. He came home alone and ate the food set for the visitors.

It was not long before he announced that four new visitors were coming. Okembe prepared a meal for four people, much to her displeasure. As always, they went to the farm.

'I think the visitors have arrived, I heard some voices.'

Okembe had expected her husband to say this.

'Go and find out,' she encouraged him.

Nambe went home and was in the process of bringing out all the meat in the soup, when his wife came in.

'Where are the visitors, Nambe?'

She picked up a club to hit her husband, but Nambe was on the alert. He ran away to the village where his mother lived. Two days after his arrival, his aged mother took ill. He suspected that she might die, and went to the elders of the village and advised them to bury his mother if she died and send him the bill afterwards. He was on a business trip, he told them. That night the mother died and the elders met and planned a course of action. A messenger was sent to tell him that his mother had grown a beard and that the Chief's sheep had grown horns. Nambe was curious over such rarities as these. He came back to his mother's village, and was confronted with his mother's corpse.

50 How man lost his tail

A long time ago human beings had long tails and were very friendly with the animals. There was at this time an epidemic in both lands – man's and the animal's – and the treatment for the epidemic was salt. A great quantity of salt was used and wasted daily and it was not long before both lands ran short of salt. Anyone who could not eat his food without salt ran the risk of being starved.

The animals could not do without salt so the elephant was sent to the land of the Spirits to buy some. To get to this market the elephant would have to pass man's land and cross two narrow bridges. Very early in the morning he set out on his mission. He met man on the way and told him where he was going and why. Man wished him good-luck. When the elephant arrived at this foreign market he found only one bag of salt. He paid double the price in order to buy it. He carried it on his back. The bag was very heavy and he had to stop at intervals to rest. After he had crossed the two bridges, he tied a rope round the neck of the salt bag and dragged it along. Man saw him coming and brought a knife.

As soon as the elephant had passed his domain, man cut the rope and carried the bag of salt away. The elephant went home and reported the theft to his brethren. They said they would declare war on man and would look for an opportunity to pay him back in his own coin.

The opportunity came when man went to a funeral ceremony held in the land of the spirits. When he was on his way back a heavy rain started. He entered a little hut where some animals were taking shelter too. He soon fell asleep and the animals cut off his long tail and ran away. When he woke up he felt for his tail but it was not there. He became tail-less.

51 *The wren and the owl*

The wren and the owl were great friends. They were very fond of each other and often made fun of themselves. One day the owl suggested that they should not eat for two market days (eight days), in order to see which was stronger than the other. The wren accepted the challenge and on the day arranged, each flew to a tall iroko tree, which was the meeting place. They would stay together in order to make sure there was no foul play.

They sang and made merry. The first day passed without any incident. On the second day the owl complained of hunger but could not call off the hunger-strike because of pride and his self-esteem. They endured their self-inflicted punishment.

On the fourth day neither of them could sing any more. The owl could not even stand up. The fifth day saw him dead.

The wren was distressed. However, he blamed his friend for remaining obstinate when he could have easily given up the challenge. He carried the carcass and went home. He ate the flesh and fashioned a whistle with the bones. The wren was a good singer and now that he had obtained a musical instrument in the form of a whistle, music became his favourite pastime.

The kite heard the melodious tunes played by the wren and came to listen. He was so enthralled by the music that he asked the wren to lend him the whistle. The wren's ego was flattered and he handed the whistle to the kite with the plea that he should return it in a few hours' time. The kite went home and gave the whistle to his aged mother.

'Hold this object for me, mother,' he told her. 'Don't give it away to anyone.'

The wren waited and waited, but it was all in vain. He went

to the kite's house where he saw the mother holding his whistle. He demanded the instrument back, but mother kite asked him to come close. She felt his body and remarked that the wren was not her son. The wren went home and covered his body with clayey soil and stuck feathers all over his body. The kite's blind mother touched him and thought he was her son. The wren went away with his whistle. When the kite came back, his mother told him she had given the whistle away.

'But I told you not to give it away, didn't I?'

He took a knife and killed her. Later on he felt a prick of conscience which made him go into voluntary exile. After an interval of nine months he came back. Even today the kite goes into exile.

52 *The true confession*

The King of the Animals announced that he had farms to be cultivated and promised to give his daughter in marriage to whichever of his subjects finished his own portion of work before the others.

The sparrow and his friend the dove, went to the King to say they were ready to work for him. There they met four other birds. The King thanked them for their interest and took them to his farms. He gave a plot of land to each of the six volunteers and asked them to come and report to him when they finished the work allocated. The six competitors worked hard. It was a hot morning and the Harmattan was blowing, but they did not mind the weather; the thought of marrying the King's daughter filled them with vigour.

They had not worked long when an old man came to them asking if any of them would come and help him to carry his bundle of firewood. Five of them refused. The old man wanted to waste their time, they said.

The sparrow pitied him and went to help him with his bundle of wood. The old man in appreciation, gave him a seed.

'Drop this on your portion of work,' he instructed the sparrow.

The sparrow did as he was bade and in the twinkling of an eye, his own plot of land was cultivated. He told his friend the dove. The latter ran to the old man and asked him to give him a seed. When the old man did not pay any attention, the dove hit him with a stick. The old man fell down dead.

He quickly covered the dead body with grass and went back to the sparrow.

'What's the point working when you've won the prize?' the dove said to the sparrow. 'Bring your gun and let's go a-hunting.'

The sparrow was an experienced hunter and gladly took his gun.

'I have no gun, I shall have to look for game for you and when I ask you to shoot, you should shoot without delay.'

They moved a little further and came to a heap of grass. The dove pointed at it and asked him to shoot. The sparrow fired. The dove removed the grass and shouted that the sparrow had killed a human being. He fled and left the sparrow behind. The sparrow was horrified. He went to the King to report that he had finished his portion of work. The King was surprised as he thought it would take them at least two days. He sent his men to go and see things for themselves. Leaving the King's palace the sparrow next went to a medicine-man.

'It was the dove who killed the old man, not you,' the medicine-man confirmed.

He brought out a royal robe and asked the sparrow to put it on. He instructed his client to go to the dove's house, and told him what to say. The dove fled when he saw the sparrow; whom he failed to recognize.

'Mr Dove, don't you know me?'

The fleeing dove came back to laugh at his own folly.

'How did you come by that flowing robe?' he asked enviously.

The sparrow sat down to answer.

'I went to the King to report the shooting incident and he praised me for ridding the community of a wizard. For my reward he presented me with this robe.'

The dove listened with interest.

'But you did not kill him, I did,' he corrected the sparrow.

He rushed to the King's palace and requested an audience with him. When the King came out, he narrated the story of the murder. He thought he would be given a prize but the King was astonished to hear the story and immediately ordered that he should be killed.

The following day he invited the sparrow to come and marry his daughter.

53 *An Unmarried Mother's song*

God, God, where are you?
   Aya – riri – Kpa
You gave me a child but no husband.
   Aya – riri – Kpa

God, God, take your child
Aya – riri – Kpa
Or else send me a husband
Aya – riri – Kpa

Child, child, who are you?
Aya – riri – Kpa
How did you manage to come?
Aya – riri – Kpa

God, God, take your child
Aya – riri – Kpa
Take your child, I'm still a virgin.
Aya – riri – Kpa

Mother, Mother, how did you get my father?
Aya – riri – Kpa
Did you get him after I was born?
Aya – riri – Kpa

God, God, you're kind
Aya – riri – Kpa
You've shown me that I'm a woman
Aya – riri – Kpa

Child, child, stay with me,
Aya – riri – Kpa
Let's wait for a man who wants us both
Aya – riri – Kpa

Men, men, where are you?
Aya – riri – Kpa
I'm waiting for any of you.
Aya – riri – Kpa

Little bird, little bird,
  Tuzanza – tuzanza
What are you doing there?
  Tuzanza – tuzanza

I'm staying here and picking nuts
  Tuzanza – tuzanza

After picking them, what next?
  Tuzanza – tuzanza

Picking over, I shall break them
  Tuzanza – tuzanza

What comes next after breaking?
  Tuzanza – tuzanza

After breaking them I'll eat them
  Tuzanza – tuzanza

Eating over, what next?
  Tuzanza – tuzanza

I shall look for more nuts
  Tuzanza – tuzanza

When you get more nuts, what next?
  Tuzanza – tuzanza

I shall sit down and break them
  Tuzanza – tuzanza

NOTE This song can go on for as many hours as the singer
wants. It is not really a song but an introduction, or 'warming-

up' that usually precedes a story. A good storyteller usually captures the attention and interest of his audience before he starts.

5 5 *The story-telling that took seven years*

Once upon a time, King Ahuho summoned all his subjects and said he wanted to hear a very long story.

'I want a story that will take three years to be told, or even a longer time.'

King Ahuho promised to give all his possessions – including his queen – to anyone who could tell such a story. The story-teller would be killed if his story finished before the end of the third year.

A month after this important announcement, a sailor named Ikeaka, went to him to say he had a story. The King invited all the members of the royal family and they sat down to hear Ikeaka's story. This was the story he told. . .

There was once a boy of fifteen who was very fond of wrestling contests. At his tender age he had defeated all the wrestlers in the village. He went to other villages to wrestle and always came home victorious. One day this boy, whose name was Nduka, came back from school and told his parents that he was going to the land of the Spirits to see if he could get a really strong opponent. His parents refused to grant him permission to go. Nduka left the house without approval and went to the land of Spirits.

He told the King what his mission was and he was given a

tough opponent. It was not difficult for Nduka to carry his opponent shoulder-high and throw him to the ground. This wrestling ground was such that any wrestler whose body touched the ground died. This meant that Nduka's opponent had been killed. The King was amazed. He doubted how a boy of Nduka's type could defeat the strongest wrestler among the spirits. He brought a horn which he placed near the ear of the dead wrestler. The dead man became alive again as soon as the horn was blown. Nduka liked the horn and smartly snatched it from the King, and ran away with it. The spirits pursued him but Nduka was too swift for them. He came home with the horn and used it to bring to life all his dead friends and relatives. . . .

At this point, Ikeaka, the story-teller, became confused. He could not continue and so the King ordered him to be killed. Other people tried but failed, and so lost their lives. A school-boy living near the King came.

'Did you tell your parents you were coming?' the King questioned him, surprised.

'My parents are all dead,' the boy answered.

'Do you know the penalty for any story-teller who fails in his attempt?'

The boy said he knew. The King asked him to go home and come back the following morning. He invited all his subjects to come and see how a little boy chose to kill himself.

That morning the King's palace was thronged with people. The little boy came and stood on a table at the centre of the hall. Be bowed and started thus:

'There was a king named Ege. He had a big store where all the maize he had been harvesting for the past twenty years was packed. It so happened that there was a little opening at the window, and through this opening a weaver-bird used to come in to carry off a grain of maize.'

The story-teller then asked his audience to answer 'Furuk-powai', whenever he said a verse which he was about to start:

> 'The weaver-bird came in
>   Furukpowai
> He carried away a grain of maize
>   Furukpowai
>
> The weaver-bird came in
>   Furukpowai
> He carried away a grain of maize
>   Furukpowai
>
> The weaver-bird came in
>   Furukpowai
> He carried away a grain of maize
>   Furukpowai.'

'What happened when the weaver-bird came in and carried away a grain of maize?' the King asked.

The story-teller answered:

> 'The weaver-bird came again
>   Furukpowai
> And carried another grain of maize
>   Furukpowai
>
> The weaver-bird came again
>   Furukpowai
> And carried another grain of maize
>   Furukpowai
>
> The weaver-bird came again
>   Furukpowai
> And carried another grain of maize
>   Furukpowai

At this stage the boy was demonstrating with his hands. At nightfall the King asked him to go home and come back the next morning. Very early in the morning he came back and started his story.

> 'The weaver-bird came in
>> Furukpowai
> He carried away a grain of maize
>> Furukpowai
>
> The weaver-bird came in
>> Furukpowai
> He carried away a grain of maize
>> Furukpowai.'

'Now tell me, my boy,' the King asked. 'What happened to the grains the weaver-bird had carried away?'

The boy answered:

> 'The Weaver-bird came in
>> Furukpowai
> And carried a grain to his house
>> Furukpowai.'

The story continued for days, then for weeks; from weeks to months and from months to years. At the end of the third year the King asked him to stop, but he wanted to continue. The story took him seven years to complete. The King gave him all his possessions including the queen.

The schoolboy story-teller then became King.

THE END